[BUTTERFLIES IN BUCARAMANGA]

TANNA PATTERSON-Z

BUTTERFLIES

A NOVEL

IN

BUCARAMANGA

NeWest Press

COPYRIGHT ©
TANNA PATTERSON-Z 2010

___ __ __

Library and Archives Canada Cataloguing in Publication

Patterson-Z, Tanna, 1955–
Butterflies in Bucaramanga / Tanna Patterson-Z.

ISBN 978-1-897126-70-7

1. Leonard, Ed–Kidnapping, 1998–Fiction.
2. Fuerzas Armadas Revolucionarias de Colombia–Fiction.
I. Title.

PS8631.A847B88 2010   C813'.6   C2010-903642-5

__ __ __

Editor: Anne Nothof
Cover and interior design: Natalie Olsen, Kisscut Design
Author photo: Gene Zackowski
Proofreading: Michael Hingston

NeWest Press acknowledges the support of the Canada Council for the Arts, the Alberta Foundation for the Arts, and the Edmonton Arts Council for our publishing program. We acknowledge the financial support of the Government of Canada through the Canada Book Fund for our publishing activities.

201, 8540 – 109 Street
Edmonton, Alberta T6G 1E6
780.432.9427
NeWEST PRESS   www.newestpress.com

No bison were harmed in the making of this book.
printed and bound in Canada   1 2 3 4 5 13 12 11 10

Thank you to Ed and Trollee, Amie and Peter
For giving me the freedom and privilege to write your story.

FOREWORD

To those who have been imprisoned, denied freedom, held captive
And presented with time to watch the ants raze a forest,
The butterfly is more than a symbol of freedom.
It is beauty, lightness, innocence,
And it is elusive.

If these yellow boots
Did not hold me to the ground
I could grasp the blue butterfly
In my hands.
Then I too,
Would be free.

To see butterflies merely as pretty objects is to miss half the story, for they are of exceptional interest in many other ways. The wings of these insects are emblazoned with the evidence of their ancestry, like the quarterings on the shields of ancient nobles.

[PAUL SMART, The Illustrated Encyclopedia of the Butterfly World]

Sweet freedom whispered in my ear
You're a butterfly
And butterflies are free to fly
Fly away, high away, bye bye.

[BERNIE TAUPIN + ELTON JOHN]

PROLOGUE

The summer before Will Edwards was kidnapped in Colombia, a medicine man told him he held the spirit of the butterfly. That was fine, but Will had participated in the healing ceremony in hopes of easing his inflamed knees, not because of an urge to fly.

Jake Across-the-Mountain was a reputable healer. People from Monarch Valley claimed that fire jumped from his hands. Jake told Will he didn't know if he could erase the effects of thirty years of hard-rock diamond drilling, but he'd give it a go. Both men agreed this was not to be a sacred sweat — Will did not wish to offend Jake by pretending he was a blood brother in search of a miracle cure. It was simply a case of bad knees bringing friends together on a late August afternoon.

By mid-ceremony, Will's concentration had crashed. With streaming eyes and a throat as dry as the sizzling juniper before him, he could no longer hear Jake moaning away in a language more akin to wind and tree than human speech. He thought only of escape, of getting outside and freeing himself from the smoke-filled tepee. When Jake revived the embers with a second handful of juniper, Will fell into a coughing fit that nearly rocked him off his fake-fur car seat cover. He began to wonder if this healing ceremony would kill him.

Will wished he could believe in the magic of the ceremony, but the ritual seemed sadly out of touch with the present day. When his mother was alive, the ancient ways held power. Her Cree medicines worked in harmony with the older, slower pace of life.

So when Jake opened his eyes and looked through his transition lenses set in their allergy-free, flexible titanium frame and asked Will to describe what he felt, Will stared back blankly. He didn't want to admit that his legs were cramping and he couldn't breathe. Jake waited. Will recalled a soft brush against his cheek, but he assumed that a sign of healing would be... well, bigger. His knees still hurt as he awkwardly hauled himself upright. He shook his head and grinned at Jake. No. Nothing.

Jake ducked out of the tepee and held the flap open for Will. Instantly revived by the flood of fresh air, Will greedily sucked buckets of air into his singed lungs. The summer sun soaked the men in gold as it slid behind the purple mountains beyond the river. They meandered along a path through Jake's backyard — a tangle of tall grasses, timothy, and wildflowers. Giant yellow swallowtailed butterflies, copper, blue, white, grey, sulphurous yellow butterflies, tiny elfin butterflies, speckled, checkered, angle-winged, frayed, and ragged butterflies surrounded them. The dusty golden light shimmered with their collective wing movement.

Jake absorbed the sight. "So it is true," he said.

Will looked at him with a raised eyebrow.

"You have the spirit of the butterfly."

Within a week, the inflammation in Will's knees subsided. He golfed a seventy-eight and got his first hole-in-one. A thousand golf swings later, Will Edwards accepted the foreman's position from the owner of a small drilling company operating in Colombia.

ONE

WILL EDWARDS emerged from the warehouse trailer into the stifling noonday heat. *How could air be this wet?* he wondered. He removed his cap and wiped the sweat from his brow with a well-muscled forearm. It was going to take more than three days to acclimatize to the heat and humidity of Colombia, even at this elevation. His head swam with details about the drilling operation he'd been hired to supervise. Was there anything else he needed to know about the job before Sam left? He turned the corner into the shade and promptly sideswiped one of three men striding toward him. He reached out in apology, then pulled back as if stung. A pistol fell from the man's hand. In a swift gesture, the man caught the gun before it hit the ground. All three men looked at a surprised Will.

— — —

Five minutes earlier, Will and the departing foreman, Sam Walters, had been inside the warehouse finalizing the details of the job they shared.

"So far, so good," Will said. "It looks like you've made my job easy."

"I don't foresee any problems, Will. This is a pretty sound operation, aside from the caving we experienced on core hole fourteen. She's tight as a hawk in a power dive now. The crew is one of the best I've worked with, and it looks like the men have warmed up to you already. Of course it helps when your brother is part of the crew — he's one hell of a driller."

Will's brother Ted was one hell of a good talker too. He was why Will had accepted this job in the first place. At age sixty, "retirement" had blundered into Will's vocabulary on occasion, but when the money and the working conditions were this amenable, the term existed only in the future tense. Will's last job in Ghana was a fading memory; it felt damned good to be working again.

"Have a good trip back to Ontario, Sam, and say hi to the family for me," Will said from the warehouse doorway. The work trailer smelled of grease and was crammed with loops of hose and wire line, spare drill rods, machine parts, and wooden crates of diamond-studded drill bits. Bags of drill mud bulged against the trailer walls. Around the perimeter, coveralls and raingear hung from three-inch spikes pounded into studs that supported the wall panelling.

"You betcha," Sam said. "It's nearly July, so the black flies ought to have chewed the ice off the lake by now. First thing on the list is to fire up the Big Merc and take the kids fishing." Sam wouldn't admit to being excited about going home, but it showed. Both men liked the idea of sharing the foreman's position because long absences tended to break up families. Six weeks from now, Will would return to his family in Monarch Valley, British Columbia, and six weeks sure beat six months. "You go ahead, Will. I'm just going to double-check these boxes of core springs and casing shoes before I go. Last time they trucked in the wrong bloody size. Catch you in the parking lot."

— — —

The three men facing Will wore their shirts loose in front of their jeans and looked uncomfortable, especially the one in the middle. Will thought his name was Armando, one of the geologists who worked for Blackburn Resources International, the Canadian mining company that established the camp and contracted out the drilling crew. Will didn't recognize the man with the uncombed grey hair and unpleasant expression, or the man he had bumped into, whose hand was now securely wrapped around his pistol. Workers in camp were not usually armed.

"*Hola*," Will said, extending a hand toward the geologist. Instead of taking it, Armando quickly told Will, "*Estos hombres son del pueblo.*" *These men are from the village.* He turned to the men and introduced Will, stressing his position as foreman of the drilling crew. All four men stood together on a piece of land that promised the company at least six million ounces of gold and over thirty million of silver. Warning bells clanged in Will's head. Colombians always shook hands.

Will looked around. Where the hell was everyone? The emptiness of the camp, especially compared to the day before, intensified Will's anxiety. Yesterday, dozens of onsite geologists studied core samples, company big shots carried briefcases, accountants and cleaning staff shuffled between camp trailers, and good smells drifted from the cook shack's open windows.

Armando continued nervously. "You are going with these men up into the hills," he said. There's been a little misunderstanding. It may take a couple of days or so to straighten things out."

Will stared hard at the small man while his palms sweated. Every worker sent to Colombia knew the country's reputation. Before Will's arrival on site, reliable sources assured him that the "patient" had been properly "vaccinated." By this, Will understood that the local guerrilla group had been paid off in exchange for worker protection against kidnapping. No, he thought, glaring at the geologist. If this were an abduction they would take Armando with them. Every worker also knew a geologist would fetch more on the black market than a driller.

The Colombian waved his pistol at Armando as if he were a fly to be shooed away.

"Ve a traer una chaqueta para este hombre," he said. Obediently, Armando hurried toward the line of camp trailers to retrieve Will's jacket from his quarters.

With the pistol now aimed at him, Will waited in silence, his anger rising. He realized how easily the little bastard had set him up. It was as clear as the call of a yellow-breasted kiskadee in an empty camp. When Armando returned with the jacket, he handed it to the grey-haired Colombian, who squeezed the pockets before handing it to Will. In an authoritative voice, the grey-haired Colombian said to Will, *"Tu vienes con nosotros."* You're coming with us.

Will took a deep breath and exhaled slowly and deliberately as Armando retreated out of reach. He watched a few drops of rain fall on the slick black hair of the man with the gun and thought he could probably use that jacket.

TWO

THERESA EDWARDS just wanted to reach the bathroom before she threw up. She grabbed the toilet with clammy hands and heaved. Rocking back onto the edge of the tub, she tucked her dark hair behind her ears and wondered what in the world could have inspired such a vivid nightmare.

In the dream, she and her sister Niyal were making strawberry jam. Niyal washed jars while Theresa skimmed the froth from the boiled fruit. An annoying gurgling sound came from the next room. It became louder — so loud that it interfered with their conversation. Theresa floated into the living room to tell it to stop. To her horror, her husband Will lay splayed out on the chesterfield, his eyes open and staring. Blood burped noisily from an x slashed through his abdomen. Theresa gaped, too stunned to scream. Tucked in beside him was their seven-year-old son Michael. Bright red blood bubbled from a similar wound cut into his narrow brown chest. She watched her son's blood flow into Will's. The viscous mix oozed down from the chesterfield and puddled into her rose-coloured carpet. Panic rolled through Theresa's watery body and slammed her into wakefulness.

On this sunny June morning in Monarch Valley, Theresa cranked open the bathroom window to allow the sweet fragrance of mock orange to fill the room. She splashed water over her face, but it refused to clean away the lingering images. The pale reflection in the bathroom mirror told her something was wrong at the mine.

THREE

WHERE WAS THE GUARD? Will stole a glance at the unmanned sentry post as he was hurried by. He carried his jean jacket in his hand and wore his coveralls over his clothes. His pantlegs were tucked into his steel-toed work boots, known throughout the drilling world as "muckers." As he passed through the camp gate, Will's muckers still had the new smell from the Monarch Valley Hardware store and shone a glossy yellow.

The sporadic raindrops suddenly turned into a violent deluge as Will was hustled into the back seat where two serious-looking men sat. "Pardon me," Will said as he climbed over a pair of long, thin legs. No response came from beneath the Aussie-style hat. The second man made eye contact and nodded as he crowded into the side of the jeep to give Will another inch. He needed twenty.

The Colombian with the pistol hovered athletically over the gear-shift next to the driver, aviator sunglasses masking his face despite the rain. The grey-haired Colombian banged his door five, six, seven times. When something finally clicked, the jeep shot off at full throttle. Will yanked his Coffin Dodgers baseball cap down over his short black hair and hugged his jacket close to his body.

— — —

As long as the jeep moved quickly, the occupants stayed dry. Will could not see past the three heads in front of him, nor could he see through the windshield, which was clear as zinc. The hiccuping wipers failed to clean the window, forcing the driver to stand several times and swipe it with his sleeve. Will leaned into his fellow passengers as the jeep skidded sideways around hairpin corners in its race down the mountain. He cussed the driver for not having the sense to lock the hubs and imagined the whole bunch of them tumbling ass over teakettle down the mountain. Decelerating only slightly, the jeep lurched onto a narrow wooden bridge that crossed the river. Below them, the agitated Rio de Oro frothed and swirled around giant boulders. Will held his breath, knowing how slippery wooden bridges can get in the rain. Seconds felt like minutes until they bumped onto solid ground again and all four cylinders strained to climb the opposite bank. Tires spun and mud flew wildly as the red rainforest muck was churned into butter.

About twenty gear-grinding minutes later, the driver rounded a blind corner and plunged the jeep into a wash of mud that blocked the road. Everyone jerked forward in unison. The driver's mirrored sunglasses crashed against the steering wheel.

Recovering instantly, the driver adjusted his sunglasses and rocked the jeep back and forth while the grey-haired Colombian seethed. Clearly exasperated, the grey-haired man climbed over the door of the jeep, followed by the armed Colombian. Will and the other two men were pistol-waved out of the back seat and told, "*Ahora, nosotros vamos a caminar.*" Now we walk.

Will brightened. Until now, he had not known the other two men were also hostages. Amid the mud splatters, the cursing, and the relentless downpour, he smiled. He was not alone.

The grey-haired Colombian left the road and surged up the mountain as if it were a city street, breaking trail through tangled vegetation that had not been buried by the mudslide. With his pistol, the second guerrilla directed Will and the others to follow.

Will looked up at the cleared mountainside. The remaining stumps looked pathetically incapable of stopping the flow of mud. He wasn't surprised the slide had occurred, just thankful it hadn't buried them when it came down. They progressed slowly. Thick vegetation concealed a litter of slippery broken logs, branches, and rocks that caused the men to stumble. Despite years of physically demanding work, Will's heart jumped around inside his chest like a caged animal as he puffed and scrambled his way up the mountain.

At the top of the slope, they reached the source of the slide, where the road had collapsed and left an impassable hole. Will thought it would continue to erode with every rainfall. On the other side of the gap the road reappeared, as did the grey-haired Colombian. He had waited only to berate the armed guerrilla for allowing the hostages to dawdle, and then he charged ahead again.

"No hablen," the armed Colombian reminded Will and the other two hostages, who had paused to catch their breath and say a few words to each other. Through his fogged and water-streaked glasses, Will looked down at the toy-sized jeep and driver, still stuck in the mud. Below the jeep, he glimpsed the Rio de Oro through the overhanging shade trees that protected its banks. On the other side of the bridge, the river snaked past the cluster of trailers that made up the Mariposa mining camp. About five hundred metres beyond the camp, Will could see the two drill sites scratched into the red earth, uncomfortably close to the river. He felt a slight nostalgia for the mining camp — it had always been a home base no matter where in the world he was. He had a feeling that this would be his last view of anything familiar for a very long time.

For some reason, Will's Native ancestry gave people license to call him names, to accuse him of stealing or cheating, and even threaten him at knifepoint. But he'd always had his freedom. But from now until his rescue, or his escape, Will would have to obey these armed men. His first challenge would be to walk in the opposite direction from his known world.

— — —

Even if they were allowed to talk, the rain pelting against the broad-leafed forest around them would have drowned out any conversation between the men. Will thought about the phone call that had brought him to Colombia.

Ted had made a ton of money when he worked for T-Rex of Timmins Drilling Company last year. He had earned more in six months in Colombia than Will made in a year chasing jobs around the world. Ted also pointed out that the company always paid on time, bonuses were bustier than a *Playboy* centrefold, and the working conditions were better than anything in Africa.

"That boss of yours is going to run out of money paying you by the hour *and* eleven dollars a metre," Will had said.

"Ha!" Ted replied. "You don't know Nick. He's the kind of guy that would run short himself before he left a worker unpaid. But he doesn't have to worry about that here. The mountains are honeycombed with gold. You ought to come down and grab a few nuggets for yourself."

"Is that why you're calling me?" Will sat down at the kitchen table and gazed out the window at his son's bike, abandoned on the front lawn. He could hear Ted drawing in his breath.

"Well, they need a drill boss. Nick's looking for a guy with experience teaching local guys how to drill. Someone who can talk Spanish. The crew is all Colombian."

There was a long pause. Bikes weren't stolen from yards very often in Monarch Valley, but Will wished Michael would get in the habit of locking it in the garage when he wasn't riding it. "You don't say."

"I told Nick I'd give you a call and see what you were up to. I think you're the right man for the job. Anything happening up there?"

"Nah. Things are slow." *Slow* euphemistically described mining in British Columbia. Drillers like Will were either doing home repairs or getting yellow fever shots and stocking up on malaria pills for Africa. *Dead* was a better word. "How's the security, Ted?"

"It's real good, Will. T-Rex has never had a problem in the five years they've been down here. I've heard the company that owns the mine has taken all the precautions. Things look top-notch. There's a fence around the camp and security guards 24/7."

Will detected the eagerness in Ted's voice as he described the skid-mounted rig, the average depth of each hole, and the dependability of the crew. "You'd share the foreman's position with another guy, so you could get home more often." Ted paused. "How would you like to be getting paid for what you're doing right now?"

Will wondered if Ted could see the potato peeler in his hand. His brother was single: no wife, no kids, no home life. No complications. Happy to have survived his past life, such as the late-night encounter on a Maracaibo highway with the cops who took a shine to their new Toyota pick-up, Will did not envy Ted. They had made it through some wild times working in places where civilization had yet to be declared. Unlike Ted, there were people in Will's life that he cared about more than himself.

Will thought about his wife Theresa. She kept a jar full of jobs for him when he was home. The new cupboards improved the kitchen, and the living room looked much bigger painted "Gentle Morning Breeze" than panelled in dark wood. When Ted had phoned, Will was at loose ends. Michael didn't have any more out-of-town hockey tournaments, so the team didn't need a driver. Kelly spent her time in the company of other twelve-year-old girls. Theresa worked full-time. Will wanted to work, and they needed the money. But Colombia? Theresa didn't like places that weren't safe.

"I'll have to talk to Theresa," he said at last. "I can't say anything for sure until then."

"Remind her that I worked here a year ago and came back with my pockets jingling," Ted said. "That's something for me. Jesus, Will, you'd have spare change even after buying that new four-by-four you've always wanted."

Money stuck to Will better than it did his brother. Two Christmases ago he'd wired cash to Ted so he could get home from New Caledonia. Ted's wages were often gone before he was.

"I'll talk to her. Where are you?"

"I'm in Bucaramanga. Remember that old hotel with the cantina? Well, the hotel is still here, but the cantina's gone. So is the three-legged dog. Oscar's nephew built a new restaurant — the food is good, and the rum's not watered down anymore. Anyway, you can get a hold of me at the Hotel California. Oscar knows me pretty good."

"I'm gonna call you back on Wednesday. Same time, okay? Give 'er some thought, Will. Nick doesn't like to wait around when there's work to do."

"Thanks for thinking about me, Ted. You stay out of trouble. I don't want my next call coming from any cement rooms without windows in downtown Bucaramanga." The brothers shared a memory that smelled badly of another time and another place.

That Wednesday, Nick Nordstrom, owner of the T-Rex drilling company, hired Will over the telephone with a two-thousand-dollar signing bonus. Will's plane ticket read June 21, two weeks after the national election in Colombia.

— — —

Will illuminated the dial on his watch. Six o'clock. The rain had stopped, but the forest continued to drip. Will's clothes were soaked as much from the exertion as from the rain. Water squelched inside his boots. He didn't know they had reached their destination until the armed Colombian told them: "*Sientence.*" The three captives sat with their backs against the same tree.

A camouflaged soldier carrying an AK-47 emerged from the forest and stood beside them. Will struggled to see into the blackness of the forest. He thought he could see more soldiers — all moving with wraithlike ease in the low light, seemingly unencumbered by their rifles and bandoliers. Awed by such a show of military hardware, Will knew escape was out of the question. He was also sure that the situation would require more than "just a couple of days to straighten out."

A cigarette thrust in his direction interrupted his thoughts. The stocky captive held the pack out to him. Will shook his head and whispered, "*No, gracias.*" The other captive eagerly accepted. Will noticed the lit end of his cigarette trembled. It could have been the cold.

Will turned toward the older captive and said, "*Mi nombre es Will Edwards.* Call me Will." For the second time that day, Will extended his hand to a man he did not know. This time, the gesture of friendship was returned.

"*Mucho gusto,*" the man said. "*Mi nombre es Luis.*" Both men smiled at each other. Luis' Spanish was that of an educated man, whereas Will's driller's Spanish reflected the language of the working class. Still, his rudimentary language skills allowed him to understand the commands of his captors and, just as importantly, to communicate with his fellow hostages. Will remembered seeing the face of freed prisoner Terry Waite on the news several years before. The Englishman tried to negotiate the release of some hostages in the Middle East and ended up a prisoner himself for years. The news reporter spoke about fear and isolation because Waite could not communicate with his tormentors or fellow captives. He had to tap on a shared cell wall — one tap for A, two taps for B, three taps for C, and so on. Will recalled how the big man laughed about having a name that required so many taps. *How in hell could he do that?*

Luis introduced the younger man, who compulsively turned his hat in his hands, as José. He paused long enough for a soft handshake, then returned to his task. Even in the dim light, his face looked pale.

"Which mine are you from?" asked Will. José shot him a hateful look.

Luis answered for José. "We're not with any mining company," he said. "I'm a metallurgist from Bolivia, and José is my apprentice, from Medellín. We are working on a river project for a Canadian environmental group in partnership with the German government."

"So why are you here?"

Luis shrugged. "I have no answer for you. My guess is that these guerrillas were 'fishing' and José and I were on the wrong river at the wrong time. This section of the Rio de Oro is in ARA territory. Our test kits and river gauges are on the bank, waiting for our return." Luis smoked his cigarette as close to his fingers as possible. "I don't expect we'll be here long, but I'm sure our gear will be gone when we get back. *Maldita sea!*" He squashed the stub against a nearby stone. They sat in darkness. "And you, Will, why are you here?"

"I'm a Canadian worker from the Mariposa goldmine."

"Oh-ho, my friend," Luis said. "Welcome to Colombia."

— — —

Will heard the approach of boots before he saw the soldier. Brown hands appeared out of a woollen cape and extended a spoon and a plastic bowl to each captive. The bowl warmed Will's hands as he looked into his rice flecked with bits of mystery meat. Then the boots retreated into the darkness. When they returned, it was to take the prisoners' bowls and announce that they needed sleep.

Accompanied by one guard, while another watched Luis and José, Will stumbled through the wet bushes in the dark to a place where he was told to urinate. He couldn't remember the last time someone watched him pee. It was a humiliating reminder of lost freedom and lost dignity. When they had all taken their turn, the hostages followed the soldiers to a stone shelter. A groundsheet and three woolen blankets were piled on the rubble-strewn floor of the shelter. When Luis spread out the groundsheet, Will thought it would be a tight fit even for three kids. He sighed, removed his wet coveralls, and rolled them into a pillow. An armed guard stood watch as the three men wrapped themselves in their own separate woollen cocoons and crowded together on the plastic sheet.

Will had spent more of his life outdoors than indoors — he was comfortable without walls around him. But he didn't remember the ground being this hard. Seven days ago he sat in his recliner watching a fishing adventure in the Scottish Highlands on TV. Aside from being damp and cold inside a crumbling stone shelter, he was as far away from a fish-filled loch as he could be. And the kid leaning against the shelter would have been holding a fishing rod instead of a loaded rifle.

Awake and alone with his thoughts, Will listened to the forest drip, soak and seep, tap and flutter, click and rustle, whine and hum. Others were in control and he couldn't do a damned thing right now to change it. But they didn't control his emotions. On this night, the first of his confinement, Will decided that there were places he would not allow his mind to go. Thinking about how Armando had betrayed him at the camp was one of those places. He would bury it, along with a thousand angry relics from the past. He shivered as the heat from his body seeped from his blanket into the stony Colombian ground. And then he thought about his wife and his family.

It would be Kelly's thirteenth birthday today... or was it yesterday? Or tomorrow? Had he lost track of time already? He recalled the apprehension in Theresa's liquid brown eyes when they said goodbye at Spokane International Airport. She was never very good at hiding her feelings. He loved his wife, and he worried about her worrying about him. He carefully placed his glasses on the ground above his head and wiped away his tears.

FOUR

A THREE-HUNDRED-DOLLAR PAIR OF LENSES soaked in the vat of tinting solution. Theresa could not understand why Mrs. Low wanted such expensive lenses coloured. She pulled the lenses from the solution with a pair of tongs and decided they needed a few more minutes. That would give her time to set the edging machine in order to cut the high-index lenses needed for the accountant's glasses. Theresa had worked at the Monarch Valley Optometry Clinic long enough to be able to shape any lens into any style of frame. She could straighten, staple, or solder eyewear that had been sat upon, driven over, chewed up, melted on the dash, twisted by grandchildren, or even blown off by a potato gun.

A telephone call broke Theresa's concentration. She would finish edging the lenses after the call. When the office manager told her it was from Colombia, her hand automatically flew to her brow. In her husband's line of work, no news was good news.

"Hello?" Her palm was moist against the receiver.

"Hi, Theresa." It was Will's brother Ted.

"Hi, Ted... Why are you calling me at work?"

"Oh, yeah, I guess it's earlier there... Sorry."

Theresa sensed the tension in his voice. Ted knew there was a four-hour time difference.

"Um...." Ted cleared his throat. "I'm not going to sugarcoat this, Theresa. Will's been taken hostage by guerrillas."

"Taken hostage?" Ted could be a jokester, but this wasn't very funny.

"I mean kidnapped."

"What?" Theresa looked in disbelief at her family photograph by the telephone.

"Will was kidnapped two days ago."

"Two days ago?" Today was Friday. That would have been Wednesday. The day of her dream. "Oh God. No! There's been a mistake. Not Will."

"We thought they'd let him go right away. But it doesn't look like that now."

Where was Will? she thought. Blindfolded, beaten up, bloodied, tied up somewhere? In a cellar, in a shed, in a ditch, in a hole in the ground? "Is he alive?" Her voice quavered. She needed to stay calm so that she could hear what Ted had to say.

"They've taken him for a reason. It's not likely they'll hurt him. We're just waiting to hear from them." To Theresa's mind, he sounded less than convinced.

"Who is 'them'?"

"The guerrillas. We know the mine was in a part of Colombia run by the revolutionary forces. We just don't have anything to go on yet."

"What exactly do they want?" Theresa wanted to sound reasonable. If only the lab wasn't so damned hot...

"Money. Usually it's money."

"Have they contacted anyone yet?" She would not cry.

"No, we're still waiting."

She pulled her shirt away from her sweating back. "Tell me what happened, Ted."

"As far as we know, two men came into camp looking for something, or somebody. Will and Sam, the foreman Will took over for, were in the warehouse, but Sam doesn't know what happened when Will left. He didn't hear a thing. No shots. No nothing. We're trying to find the geologist who's gone AWOL since Will disappeared. He might know more." Theresa heard Ted stub out his cigarette, then the click of his lighter. "You gotta believe me when I say this, Theresa, but I wish they'd taken me."

Me too. Did she say that out loud? God, she hoped not. Ted was hurting. She could not be angry with him.

"What do we do?" Theresa's voice was small. "What's going to happen to him?"

"They'll probably hold him for a couple of weeks, then let him go." Ted's voice became hard-edged. "Blackburn's still quiet on the matter. I think the company assumed the workers would get over it. But I know the men aren't going back until Will's safe at camp. Everyone here likes Will."

Theresa didn't hear the last words. What was Blackburn again? Things were becoming muddled. Was Will in pain? "When will you know anything?"

"No one knows. I think we just wait until they're ready to tell us." She heard Ted blow out his smoke. "Look, I'll call you tomorrow. Nick's on his way. He'll know what to do."

Theresa was unsure who Nick was. "How do I tell the kids?" Tears pooled in her eyes.

Ted waited a long time before answering. "Tell them they're not going to hurt him." The kids loved Uncle Ted. "Is there anyone that could stay with you and the kids tonight?" Theresa's tears rushed down her hot cheeks when she thought how hurt the kids would be when she told them the news.

"Do you think you're going to be all right, Theresa?"

"Yes — no, I'm not going to be all right." Even when Will first told her about the big pay he'd be earning in Colombia, Theresa suspected there had to be risks.

"This is going to take time," Ted reminded her. "Nothing's going to change overnight — but I promise to call if we hear anything. Anything."

"Call even if you don't hear anything."

"Sure thing, Theresa." Neither of them spoke. A silent telephone line is as empty as a street with no people. Still, Theresa hung on. She didn't want to let go of Ted, but there was nothing left to say.

"Take care," he said.

"You too," she said. "Goodbye."

Theresa held the dead receiver and stared into space. Should she call Will and Ted's sisters? She looked over at the tinting vat — ohmigod — Mrs. Low's lenses! Theresa reeled. Where were her tongs? Where *in hell* were her tongs? She pulled open all the drawers and slammed them shut. Fuck! She needed her tongs! Who put her tongs next to the tinting vat? She whipped the lenses out. They stared back her, the colour of steeped tea. Theresa slumped into her chair in front of the edging machine that had slipped an unacceptable three degrees and started to bawl.

The office manager, the doctors, and staff crowded into the lab. Justine, Dion, Kristin, and Bridgette all hugged Theresa until Niyal arrived to take her home. In Niyal's car, Theresa sobbed, "I can't go home yet. The kids will be there. I don't want them to be as scared as I am. I want to give them hope."

Niyal circled the block while Theresa talked and cried. "Will always called me when he reached his destination," she said. "The last time he called, it was from the camp. He told me to tell everyone at his office that he'd be back for the Labour Day golf tournament. You know how he calls the golf course his office? Anyway, he sounded so happy. He told me not to worry about him because security looked good. He knows I can tell if he's fibbing, so he must have truly believed the camp was safe." Theresa blew her nose. Niyal drove around the block one more time before she coasted into the Edwards driveway.

— — —

"To freedom!" Kelly Edwards clinked her glass against Kat's. The girls had spiked their lemonade with a pinch of Will's rum. After all, it was the last day of school. And Kelly had just turned thirteen! Their favourite soap blared from the TV in the living room. When Kelly noticed her mom in her aunt's Jetta outside, she screwed the cap back on the rum bottle and stuffed it to the back of the cupboard.

"Shit! Mom's home. Where's that list of things to do she left on the table?"

The girls rushed through their chores in a matter of seconds. Kat gathered popcorn kernels and dirty dishes and dumped them in the kitchen sink. Kelly ran downstairs, loaded the dryer, ran back upstairs two at a time, picked up the dog's bowl, rinsed it over the dishes, and heaped it up with Kibbles 'n Bits. "*Snorrrrrrr-ty!*" she yelled into the backyard. A cocker spaniel-like mutt bounded through the back door to his bowl.

Kelly turned around to see Niyal open the front kitchen door. Theresa followed, her eyes downcast. Kelly's face turned pasty white. When Theresa looked at Kelly, a flood of tears gushed out. She went to her daughter and hugged her so hard that it hurt. Theresa cried into Kelly's dark hair: "Dad's been captured by guerrillas."

"Oh no, not my Dad!" Kelly slumped in her mom's arms.

"Kelly! Kelly!" Theresa eased her into a chair and patted her cheeks. Kat squeezed Kelly's hand. Niyal fetched a glass of water as Kelly came to, whimpering. "Is he dead? Is he ever coming home?"

Theresa tried to be calm. "Dad's not dead and Uncle Ted says they're not going to hurt him. They've taken him for a reason." Theresa felt like an atheist reciting the Lord's Prayer at a funeral.

Niyal placed the full teapot next to the Kleenex box and told everyone to sit down at the table. They sat while she poured. Everyone looked into their teacups, but there were no answers. At last, the telephone fixed to the kitchen wall rang.

Theresa answered. "Hello — ?"

"Nick Nordstrom here. T-Rex of Timmins Drilling Company." Theresa held the receiver away from her ear. Everyone seated at the table could hear the assertive voice. "Mrs. Edwards?"

"It's Theresa." She twisted the telephone's long, curly cord with her free hand.

Nick continued, loudly. "I am really truly sorry for what's goin' on with Will. Christ almighty, Mrs. Edwards, I'm more surprised about this kidnapping than anyone. I feel like I bin slugged in the gut. Your husband's a damned good man."

Theresa had never seen Nick Nordstrom, the owner of the drilling company, nor heard his ferocious voice prior to this telephone call. She knew him only as the man who hired her husband for the job in Colombia.

"The guerrillas are not gonna hurt Will. Not 'cause they're nice guys, but because he's worth more to them alive than dead," Nick bellowed. "Things in Colombia have been goin' to hell in a handbasket since their national election and I can't get a good goddamned flight outta Toronto 'til after the weekend. Meanwhile, I'll give you my number in Timmins in case you wanna get a hold of me." Niyal placed a pen and paper on the table. Nick's voice was loud and clear.

"Why didn't you call two days ago?"

"We thought it would sort itself out in a coupla days. But things didn't happen like we thought they would." Theresa wondered if Nick and Ted had practiced their lines together before they spoke to her. "I'm gonna figger out this whole frickin' mess, pardon me, as soon as I get down there. After doin' business down there for five years, I know how things work in Colombia, and I know people who can help." Nick paused to catch his breath. "I'll find a way to get Will home."

Theresa's eyes welled up with tears again. She was desperate to believe this man, but would his actions speak as loudly as his words? Nick then told her he had contacted Foreign Affairs in Ottawa and they would call her soon. He also promised to call her from Colombia. Monday. He hung up with a bang.

Niyal told Theresa to keep a record of her phone calls and write down her questions in a book. Before Theresa could respond, the phone rang again. She answered, and after a few seconds held the receiver away while she whispered to the others, "It's Foreign Affairs."

Theresa sighed with relief. Her husband, an innocent man hired to do a job, was kidnapped by guerrilla forces in a foreign country. Thank God the Canadian government — a government she could trust with all her heart, a country with a Charter of Rights, a good country that would never kidnap anyone, a country with a safety net that cared about each one of its citizens no matter where in the world they were — had called to help.

The man, who introduced himself as James Litchfield, spoke slowly, as if his words were being recorded. "Now Mrs. Edwards," he said, "our country has a policy that we do not support the activities of terrorist organizations. I want you to see this from our perspective. Our ministry excludes terrorists from the realm of negotiation because payments of millions of dollars only encourage the terrorists to kidnap more people."

Theresa didn't speak. His conversation sounded scripted, and she didn't care for the patronizing tone. When Litchfield told her, "Your husband's situation steps beyond the scope of Foreign Affairs. Simply put, we don't talk to terrorists," she felt herself in free fall. She reached across the table for Kelly's hand.

"We will negotiate with the proper Colombian government officials on this," Litchfield continued. "We can't overrule their existing framework of law enforcement and just send someone in to pull your husband out. It's very important that you allow us the time we need to do our work. Please do not go to the media, as the media can make things worse for the detainee. Our department is trained in diplomacy. The media is not. In fact, the media could damage our relations with Colombia. International relations are very delicate, and you know as well as I do that reporters will say anything to make a good story."

Theresa grabbed at a Kleenex and blew her nose. She had no questions and Litchfield did not encourage asking any.

"This is going to take a very long time. We need you to be patient while we work this through. Any media contact could jeopardize your husband's safety."

Theresa stared glassily at old Snorty's bowl on the kitchen floor.

"Didn't your husband consult our official travel advisory before he agreed to work in Colombia?" Litchfield asked. "Foreign Affairs and International Trade Canada have advised against all travel to the *departmentios* of Arauca, Choco, Norte de Santander, and Santander. Rural Santander, especially, has been flagged in red at 'Avoid All Travel,' the fourth level of precaution issued to travellers when there is a threat of terrorism, civil unrest, war, rebellion, or political instability. Guerrilla groups are active in the area; they perpetrate attacks, extortion, kidnappings, and there may be landmines. Plus, Mrs. Edwards, it is hurricane season until the end of November. Let me assure you that the Government of Canada closely monitors safety and security conditions abroad, and advisories are updated regularly. We recommend that all workers follow our advisories."

"Yes," Theresa said vaguely.

"Then why did you let him go?"

A bad feeling had always surrounded the job in Colombia. Theresa had been a driller's wife long enough to know the contract's unwritten clause: more money meant more danger. While Will considered Colombia, she reminded him of their two children. But a man has to work. Honestly, how many more jobs around the house could she get him to do? She knew he preferred mucking around in the drilling field to stuffing chickens. How could she say no to Will based on a feeling? At the close of the conversation, Theresa felt terrible. And she felt guilty. Why *had* she let Will go?

"*Fu-uck*," she whispered in disbelief as she hung up the phone.

"What, Mom?"

She turned to the faces looking in her direction. "It's going to take time. He didn't tell me what they could do. They told me I shouldn't have let him go. Oh, and I shouldn't talk to the media." She paused. "When did we start calling guerrillas 'terrorists'?"

As she looked at her older sister, she saw their mother. Fleetingly, she wished her mother were alive to help her through this. Niyal returned the look. It was the same expression she wore in last Wednesday morning's awful dream.

"What should I do?" Theresa's words sounded like they were underwater.

— — —

Minutes later, Michael burst into the house as blithely as Tigger bounding through Rabbit's rutabaga patch. He carried the last remnants of Grade Two in his backpack and his mind was full of summer holiday plans. First thing was to meet Brennan at the swimming pool. He didn't have time to sit at the table with these stern-faced women. Even when they told him about his dad, he could not understand why everyone was so glum. Why would gorillas kidnap his dad? How would they fit their big hairy fingers around the trigger of a gun? Once someone lassoed all the gorillas and put them back in their cages, his dad would come home and tell them all about it. Just like he always did.

That evening, Theresa's brother-in-law, Uncle Bud, kept Michael company. He'd been crying off and on all afternoon and didn't eat any supper. Niyal watched TV with Kelly all night because she would not go to bed. Theresa lay awake, cold and lonely in her queen-sized bed, half-listening to the TV in the living room. She thought about the family reunion planned for Canada Day weekend that Niyal convinced her not to cancel. She was probably right when she said, "We can all sit together and worry instead of sitting alone and worrying." Tomorrow she and Niyal would buy an answering machine that would record incoming calls as well as messages. It would signal long-distance call waiting with two beeps.

— — —

The news of Will's kidnapping spread through Monarch Valley like a nasty virus. Theresa avoided going downtown, as she had become its dark celebrity. She just wanted to stay home and wrap her family around her. That's why, instead of buying groceries, she found herself standing on a ladder nailing wooden butterflies to the front of the house. Proud of the butterflies he'd painted in school, Michael chattered away: "There's one each. You get the big orange one. Do you like the yellow eyes? Kelly gets the green and pink one. I smudged it here, but it's still okay, right, Mom? And I get the red one. Mr. Scott says red is a strong colour. Can you nail me up higher than Kelly, Mom?"

"But Michael, you've got three butterflies and there are four of us. What about Dad?"

Michael thought a bit. "I think Dad has his own butterfly with him." Theresa stopped in mid-hammer and looked at her son. Michael's thoughts changed direction and he said, "I know. We can pretend the Dad butterfly is in the rabbit cage."

"Well, I think you and I better get Dad out of the rabbit cage. Why don't you ask Mr. Scott if you could paint another one for Dad during the summer holidays?"

"Okay, Mom. But can I hammer him?"

Before Theresa could answer, the phone rang for the fifth time.

FIVE

A STIRRING IN THE PRE-DAWN MIST alerted Will to morning. That
and the crescendo of bird calls. It had been one of the longest nights
Will could remember and he was glad it was over. Questions as hard
as the ground beneath his aching hips had kept him from sleeping.
What were they planning to do with him? If there was no money,
would they kill him? Throughout the long night, Will thought about
death and he thought about life. He was not a young man anymore,
and he had enjoyed his sixty years of adventurous and rewarding life.
Perhaps he had not accumulated the trappings of wealth, but he had
found love, and for that, he could die a happy man. But not yet. He
wanted to see his kids mature into adulthood. He vowed to survive
this ordeal for them.

The shadowy figures tended to early morning tasks soundlessly as if they lived in the presence of a predator. Will reached for his glasses and checked his watch. Six o'clock. Day and night were equal a mere seven degrees north of the equator. As stealthy as the bandits before his eyes, he watched the light of day kill the darkness and felt the warmth of the sun chase away the mist. Maybe this new day would bring answers to his long night of questions.

The guard also looked at his watch. He then spoke aloud to the captives — it was time for something to eat. Shivering and draped in their blankets, Will, Luis, and José followed him to the camp stove. Will limped with a stiff back and an uncooperative hip. He hoped the stove might give off some heat. It didn't. The soldier tending the one-burner Coleman stove gave them the same bowls they had last night filled with the same rice and... pork. He dipped three plastic mugs, one at a time, into a pot of tepid water, sprinkled instant coffee granules over the top, and handed a mug to each captive. Will nodded a thanks to the soldier. Surrounded by the world's richest and most aromatic coffee beans, Will sipped from his mug of coffee spooned from a plastic tub of Nescafé.

José looked at his bowl of rice and dumped it on the ground. "I'm not eating that shit," he said.

Luis frowned, and Will told José he should eat because he needed to keep his strength up. The cook didn't offer a second choice.

As Will ate his dry rice, he counted guerrillas. There didn't seem to be as many as last night, and judging by the acne and sparse whiskers, today's soldiers were considerably younger. Daylight also revealed that four of the soldiers were girls — maybe fifteen or sixteen years old. Will counted twelve of them altogether, including the grey-haired commander and the pistol-wielding second-in-command. The commander was clearly army-trained, but, Will wondered, which army? And what drove him to a life outside the law? Revenge? Frustration? Control? A Castro-like vision of riding an army tank through Bogotá cheered by an adoring crowd? The soldiers didn't seem to share their leader's zeal. To Will, they looked too young to be driven by anything except hormones. This could be a schoolyard where kids carried assault rifles instead of notebooks.

After Will, Luis and José rinsed their bowls and spoons in the stream, they sat in the shade to escape the sun's searing heat. Will asked their guard how he should address the commander. The boy soldier didn't seem to understand his question. Will blamed his foreign-sounding Spanish and asked again, "What do you call him? El Capitán?" He took the boy's shrug as a yes. El Capitán he would be.

As if summoned by the one-sided conversation, El Capitán approached the three men with his arms full of gear. Each prisoner was given a well-used backpack and items that might encourage personal hygiene: extra articles of clothing, including socks and underwear, toothbrushes, hand soap, laundry soap, towels, and a roll of toilet paper. El Capitán then looked at their footwear. The boots Luis and José wore passed inspection, but Will's muckers did not. Orders were given to the second-in-command. Minutes later, the second-in-command returned with a pair of black heavy-soled rubber boots. Will appeared doubtful and showed El Capitán that the size ten boot did not fit his size twelve foot. And no, he would not cut the toes off. The young male soldiers that had gathered pointed to Will's large feet and sniggered. El Capitán was not amused. Impatiently, he gave the order to move out. "*Vámonos!*" Will pulled on his shiny yellow muckers, glanced up at the boy soldiers, and grinned from ear to ear.

The guerrillas had dismantled everything and divided the contents of the camp equally among themselves. They hoisted their packs onto their backs as if lifting sacks filled with bird songs. Will guessed that each soldier carried about sixty pounds of gear. Unfortunately, the weight distribution was less even between the captives. José, younger and thinner than Will and Luis, refused to carry the groundsheet or the latrine shovel. Will did not think Luis should assume the burden, so he shoved both items into his backpack. The shovel was heavy, and the groundsheet so bulky that Will had to fill his pockets with items the pack would not hold. He strapped on his pack and stood ready for whatever might come next.

Vámonos. Not where, not when, not for how long, and not why. El Capitán set a brisk pace, and was out of sight within minutes. The second-in-command, handgun screwed into the waistband of his fatigues, then assumed the lead. José followed, then the soldier wearing a Che Guevara headscarf, then Will, then another soldier, and then Luis. The remaining eight soldiers and the pack mule followed at the back. There was no talking, no complaining, no slowing down, and no tolerance for slacking.

Just as the soldiers watched him, Will watched them right back. They seemed orderly and well disciplined, but their faces were dull. Each soldier hung grenades, spare clips of ammunition, knives, and an occasional machete from their belts. They walked with their rifles cradled in their arms. Their camouflage fatigues and caps were almost new, and their boots were in good repair. This gave Will some relief. At least his captors were not an overarmed bunch of nervous renegades out for a cash grab — it was a well-supplied, well-organized, well-disciplined army out for a cash grab.

Thinking and walking complemented each other, as if the mind were designed to travel at the same speed as the feet. Will's mind wandered back to the scene of the abduction. Why was the mining camp so empty that afternoon? Did Blackburn know the guerrillas were coming? If so, why in hell weren't the drillers tipped off? What about the company's "vaccination"? What was happening back at the mine site? Did Sam go home? Ted must be worried. What about Theresa? Goddamn it all to hell! He focused on the route ahead and thought about escape.

Months without rain had made the path hard. It had been worn into the ground by people and animals, connecting farmhouses to fields of maize, plantain, and cassava, and to plantations of coffee, coca, and marijuana. They often passed workers on the trail as they walked. The *campesinos* would gaze downward at their leather hands wrapped around their manual tools, careful not to show interest in the passing brigade.

Will's hips reminded him with every step that it had been many years since he'd donned a pack and walked up and down mountains. The latrine shovel dug into his side. The pack did not fit his back and rubbed against his shoulders. Adjusting the straps only exchanged one sore spot for another. He sweated as he'd never sweated before. Drops fell like machine-gun fire from the band of his hat over his face. It poured down his back, soaked his underwear, and continued down his legs, where it pooled in his boots. Mosquitoes and flies attracted to the sweat constantly annoyed him. When the troop came to a shady place near water, the second-in-command called for a break. Will and Luis dumped their packs and collapsed against them.

José dropped his pack about three metres away, turned his back to Will and Luis, and reached for his cigarettes. Unimpressed by José's lack of cooperation, Will asked Luis, "What in hell's with him?"

Luis whispered, "José is afraid. He is from a poor Colombian family and he's not worth as much money to the guerrillas as we are." They watched José try to strike a deal with the guard over cigarettes. "Fear is a great motivator. It makes people do things they wouldn't normally do. Or admit to doing."

Will respected Luis' view. "This is all about the money, isn't it?"

"*Sí*. It's extortion. The guerrillas want money. Great amounts of money. Unfortunately, or fortunately, depending upon which end of the South American gun you are on, someone will come through for us. Money will appear from your company. It always does. Money will appear from the German government or the conservation group that hired José and me. And it can't happen soon enough, because every day without freedom is a long day."

Speech required energy that Luis lacked. "If you live in Bogotá and want to see an end to a decades-old war," he continued wearily, "you don't want governments or companies caving in to guerrilla demands. But when it's you, it's much easier to bargain away what you believe in to survive. Nothing succeeds like success, my friend. Money allows the guerrillas to buy more guns and ammunition. Some trickles down to schools, medicines, environmental restoration, for people living in the country that the government ignores." Luis closed his eyes, as tired physically as he appeared to be politically. "The government calls them names. 'Terrorist' seems fashionable these days. Then they say, 'We don't talk to terrorists.' Without dialogue, there is no hope of resolution, and the war goes on."

As he listened, Will watched the soldiers fill their canteens and light their cigarettes. Some dozed against the giant shade trees. The sound of the stream and the coolness of the breeze reminded him how drained he felt. Before his eyes closed, he saw two blue butterflies dart from sunlight to shadow by the stream. *If only they would lend him some of their energy — just enough to get through the day*, he thought before drifting into sleep.

The next thing he knew, the soldier with the Che Guevara headscarf was shaking him awake. Will hurt all over, but he felt refreshed. Through a leafy overhead lattice, Will noticed that massive cumulus clouds now covered the sun. He helped Luis with his pack, donned his own wet pack, and fell into formation. José's aloofness and his refusal to assist anyone aggravated Will because he knew that surviving captivity was like climbing a mountain. Its success depended upon people working together.

As the afternoon wore on, the clouds continued to pile into tall, unsteady towers until finally they toppled in a thunderous downpour. The troop paused so that the soldiers and captives could wrap their rain ponchos and groundsheets around themselves. A sudden crack of thunder spooked the supply mule. Everyone watched it jerk away from its handler and gallop down the hill toward a farm, sacks of dry goods and kitchen utensils flapping. The soldier girl at the end of the formation dropped her pack and raced after the animal.

Amazed by the speed and agility of the girl with the long black braid, Will knew he would not be able to outrun the soldiers if he tried to escape. He would have to find another strategy — perhaps his age could be used to his advantage. He decided he would grunt and puff audibly on any uphill climb, demonstrating to his captors that this was a great hardship for a man his age. He wouldn't even have to act all that much. When the opportunity to escape arose, he would run up the mountain, and they would look for him down the mountain because that would be expected of him. Sometimes a headstart was all you needed in life. In the meantime, he followed the Che headscarf in front of him; the wearer's name was Francisco.

The troop travelled through the rain, aiming northeast. Because they were in the mountain's valleys and not on top of them, Will couldn't get an aerial view of the landscape. Twice he heard airplanes overhead. He detected a change in the engine, as they descended into what must be Venezuela, twenty or thirty kilometres away. Thanks to a childhood spent out of doors, a built-in compass, and a memory for landscapes, Will could never get lost. He thought about the time he and his brother tracked the fish and game officer, stole his boat, and went for a cruise on Great Slave Lake. Will found his way home, but a search party was sent out for the officer.

Two hours before sundown they made camp. Will was exhausted. They must have hiked twenty kilometres through morning heat and afternoon downpour. He watched the soldiers set up the army pup tents and the camp kitchen. They cooked enough rice, beans, *plátanos*, and tortillas for fifteen equal portions. Will ate his share and noticed José spoon down his own without complaint.

Luis and José crawled into their tent, but Will sat on the ground outside, a few metres away from their guard. He opened a small two-by-four-inch logbook that he kept in the pocket of his coveralls to record the progress of each drill at the Mariposa mine site. The numbers — s198-14, s198-15, s198-12, depth in metres and inclination in degrees — were now meaningless. He flipped to a new page and pulled a pencil stub from the coil binding. The thin crescent of the moon shone through the trees. He recorded the date and the day's events and then returned the book to the safety of his coveralls pocket. A calendar would remind him of days past, and days to come. It was also a statement of acceptance of his situation and the fact that he was definitely in it for the long term.

Will hauled off his boots, which had lost some of their gloss and all of their new smell. Mechanically, he rubbed his tired feet and wondered how he could dry his socks and keep them from falling down as he walked.

When he looked up, the soldier girl with the long black braid stood between him and the guard. How long had she been there?

"*Hola,*" Will said.

With a smooth brown hand, she held out a can of foot powder. She was smaller than his daughter Kelly. Will thanked her for the talcum. Now the tops of his boots wouldn't chafe his legs when his socks slipped down. He grinned at her. "I may need this when it's my turn to run away."

She understood his Spanish and smiled at the ground with even white teeth and then slipped back into the jungle.

— — —

Will ducked into the tent, yanked his coveralls out of his pack, and began to remove his clothes. He heard José grumble, "This filthy groundsheet is still wet. And I'm cold."

"It's your clothes that are wet, not the groundsheet," Will said.

"Right. And yours aren't?"

"Yes they are, but during the day, I keep my coveralls in my pack. Now I have something dry to sleep in."

Luis laughed out loud. "You mean you have something more comfortable to slip into."

"I know you're both jealous of my pajamas. You see, it's cold up here and I'm nice and dry," Will replied.

It was the first time José had spoken to Will, and the first time Luis laughed. Together they had survived day one. Less fearful but more tired than the night before, José and Luis soon fell asleep. Will rolled from one hip to the other. At least sleeping shoulder-to-shoulder with two guys was warm. Despite their differences in education and background, he and Luis could talk about work experience and family life. José, on the other hand, showed less maturity than the young soldiers. The one redeeming thing about him, Will thought, was the deck of cards he carried in his pocket. Perhaps some gin rummy might make José, and this whole bad experience, a little more tolerable.

SIX

"BANG!"

"Gotcha!"

"I gotcha first."

"No, ya didn't. Bang! Bang!"

"Yeah, I did. Take that! Bang!"

"Argh, I've been hit!"

There was no safe place. Guerrillas hid behind every tree in the forest. Michael rolled off his bike and hit the earth. Wincing with pretend pain, he fired his gun a few more times, then crawled on his elbows and knees for cover. He crouched in the bushes so the guerrillas wouldn't see him, made a run for his bike, jumped on, and raced through the woods to catch up to Brennan. Guerrillas always tailed him. Good thing he had a bike that ripped so fast they never caught up. Except at night. He would ask his mom to check under the bed just to make sure — you never knew when a big guerrilla might show up — even though she said guerrillas didn't live in Monarch Valley. He flew over a jump and crashed down on another couple of guerrillas. Which way did Brennan go?

Michael hollered into the trees, "*Bren-nan*! The guerrillas just about got me back there!" There was no reply. He pedalled crazily until he saw a flash of his friend's jacket through the trees. "Hey, Brennan! Wait up!"

He was mad at Brennan because he'd said there was no way he would pay a million bucks for his dad. Michael figured his dad was worth a lot more than a million — maybe a billion, or a zillion. In fact, he told Brennan, his dad cost way beyond money. How could anyone say this person costs a million, and that person costs $4.50? Horses and some people's dogs cost money. Not people. Except bad guys on wanted posters. And his dad was not a bad guy. Just to get even, Michael told Brennan he couldn't borrow his bike helmet with the glow-in-the-dark visor ever again.

— — —

While Michael and Brennan evaded guerrillas outside, Kelly stewed in the kitchen. Should she go to the beach with Kat and Gillian? Her mom was especially crabby these days and told her to go. "This kidnapping thing is not going to be resolved overnight," she said. "You may as well go out with your friends and try to have a good time."

"Good time?" Kelly said dramatically. "How am I supposed to have a good time with Dad held prisoner somewhere?" She cried for him day and night, and hoped with all her heart that they were not being mean to him. She wondered what he got to eat and if he remembered her birthday four days ago.

Speaking of birthdays, she'd just had the worst one in her whole life. Mom didn't want kids around the house in case the phone rang, so Kat invited everyone to her house for a sleepover. Kat's brother and his friend Darren were goofing around with big water guns — bugging the girls, of course. Kelly told her mom later that night she could have handled the gun thing, but when Darren grabbed Kat and held her hostage — well, that's when she freaked. Darren must have been the only guy in Monarch Valley who didn't know what happened to her dad.

— — —

Since last Friday's phone call from Ted, Theresa had experienced a vile brew of emotions: fear, helplessness, guilt, frustration, confusion, anger, and melancholy. Nights without sleep ruined her days. She worried about Michael and Kelly, about missing work, but mostly about Will. Friends, and anyone who wore glasses, it seemed, called to give support and offer help. People from the neighbourhood brought enough casseroles, squares, loaves, flowers, and fruit baskets to feed all the O'Neills at an Irish wake. Or all the Edwardses at a family reunion.

"Sweet Jesus," Theresa muttered as she looked at the kitchen calendar. Tomorrow was Friday. Family members would be arriving for the weekend. The guest bed cried out for fresh sheets. The bathroom refused to clean itself. The screen door still hung at an angle. Michael's backpack lay where he dropped it a week ago, and the cupboards were hungry. And there was no beer. Whether they were laughing in it or crying in it, Will's relatives liked their Monarch Valley-brewed beer.

Theresa jumped when the phone rang. Her nerves were as sensitive as ingrown toenails. So when Ted asked, "How are you and the kids doing?" he got a blast.

"Kelly mopes around and cries at the drop of a pin, Michael's imagination wakes him up at night, my husband could be dead, and I feel like I'm riding some hellbound runaway train," she said. "Oh, and guess what? The bridge is out and company's coming. If the phone rings one more time tonight, I'm going to rip it off the wall!

Tell you what, Ted. I'll ask how you're doing instead. What the hell is going on down there?"

Ted noted the edge in Theresa's voice. "Um... we haven't heard anything from anyone."

"Who's 'anyone'?"

"We all figure it's the ARA."

"What's the ARA?"

"Arauca Revolutionary Army. It's the main guerrilla group in northeast Colombia. They control everything outside of the major cities from the Arauca River — the river that marks the Venezuelan border — pretty well to Bucaramanga. Blackburn's mines are right smack in the middle of their territory."

"Well, that's just great. What do you mean 'control everything'?"

"They're in charge. If you set up business in the territory they've claimed, you pay them money. It's their taxation system. If they think you cheated them, then they come for you."

"Oh. Sounds simple enough. Is it a big group? I mean, how well-organized are they?"

"Yeah, the ARA is one of the biggest guerrilla groups in Colombia — could be twelve to fifteen thousand, people say. There's no hard numbers. And they're damn well organized. Some of the other groups that aren't so organized just kill hostages to get attention. Damn it! Sorry Theresa, I shouldn't have said that. Anyway, with the ARA, it's a matter of money."

"Are they violent? Would they torture Will, or chain him up in some tin shack?"

"No, they're not like that. They started out like the Robin Hoods of the woods, you know, steal from the rich and give to the poor. I think the drug business is involved now, but I don't know for sure. It's kind of hard not to be in the drug business in Colombia. Kidnapping is very lucrative for them — besides mine workers, they like to set up roadblocks in the rural areas and collect foreigners for ransom. Anyway, they'll take care of Will until they get their money."

"How much money?" With a pang of guilt, Theresa thought about her house: it was on a crescent beside a park — much newer and more spacious than the one she grew up in.

"No idea. We're still waiting for some communication from them."

Theresa sighed. The dishwasher swished and thumped noisily. "What made you think it was safe, Ted?"

"Blackburn Resources International was supposed to have paid protection fees to the guerrillas. They hire the drilling companies. This was a big contract for T-Rex, you know. We were told not to worry."

"You're not still at work on the site, are you?"

"Blackburn wanted us guys to keep working but we said to hell with that. It wouldn't take long for the guerrillas to find out that everything was hunky dory, and then they'd really be pissed. Will would be shot at sunrise. The guys think too much of Will to let that happen. I'd say half of them went home already."

"Where's the money going to come from?" How she loved her house and the big garden in the backyard and her rosebushes and colourful flowerbeds in the front.

Bloody hell! She shouldn't be thinking so selfishly about her house and all the happy memories it held. But she couldn't stop herself. She knew if she had to sell, she would. Thankfully she and Will owned a house that could be used as collateral and converted to freedom.

"Um... that's a good question. We figure Blackburn should do the honourable thing and come through with the cash. They've got the deepest pockets of anyone involved. T-Rex doesn't have the money to pay straight out."

"It's Blackburn's gold mine, isn't it?"

"Yeah, but I'm not sure Blackburn will pay anything."

"What?"

"They don't figure they're responsible for contracted-out T-Rex workers."

"You've got to be kidding. I mean, shouldn't the company whose name is on the deed be responsible? Surely Blackburn's concerned about safety for their workers."

"In an ideal world," Ted mumbled, wondering how women always knew when they weren't told everything. "I have to tell you this, Theresa. Remember Sam, the other foreman? He said when they took off with Will the camp was pretty near empty."

Theresa was puzzled. "So?"

"It was like everyone knew something was up. Except the drillers."

"You mean Blackburn knew the guerrillas were coming?"

"Well, all we know is that Blackburn's high-paid guys weren't there."

"Holy shit," Theresa whispered into the phone. She heard Ted's cigarette squash into the ashtray again. She could see the saggy bed he was sitting on in a tiny smoke-filled room. "There's a man's life at stake here. Isn't that more important than money? Will's getting on in years. Lots of stuff could happen to him in the jungle."

"I know."

The dishwasher shut down with a bang. "What about the government? Isn't there a Canadian embassy down there? Surely *they* care if innocent people get kidnapped. And Will *is* innocent."

"There's no embassy here. Nick and me, we'll talk to the embassy in Bogotá. But you know what, it makes more sense to talk to the ARA directly. They're holding all the cards. We're just swatting flies in the dark 'til we hear from them."

Theresa turned the light on over the kitchen sink and began to empty the dishwasher. "Some newspapers have called me," she said. "*Vancouver Sun, Globe and Mail, Ottawa Citizen, Calgary Herald.* What do I tell them?"

"Don't say anything."

"That's what Foreign Affairs told me."

"Everything's touchy right now. The next little while is real crucial. We don't need any foreign journalists messing up negotiations."

Theresa heard the sadness in his voice. She didn't want to lay any more guilt on him. She felt sorry for Ted. She sighed. "Where are you now?"

"Bucaramanga."

Theresa imagined a crowded, diesel-filled Latin city on the equator — so different from her quiet mountain town with four distinct seasons. "What are you going to do there?"

"Nick's here. He's got ideas. We'll work something out."

"At least Nick seems to care about Will. I haven't heard anything from Blackburn. What if the guerrillas ask for more money than Nick's company can pay?" She thought of her house once more with guilt-laden fondness. "They won't hang onto Will indefinitely. Especially if he gets sick."

"I don't know, Theresa. Nick'll work something out. We'll call you."

Theresa had less confidence in Nick's ability to "work something out" than Ted did. But Nick promised he would find a way to get Will home. And that was more than anyone else had done. "Nick sounds like he knows what's going on down there. Keep me informed, okay? No more waiting two days before you call. I want to know as soon as something happens."

"Sure thing, Theresa. I'm sorry about all of this shit. I'll call tomorrow. In fact, I'll call every night at this time. Does that sound okay?"

"Yes, I would really appreciate that. So would Kelly and Michael. Take care of yourself and Nick down there."

"Yeah, you too, Theresa. Give those kids a big Uncle Ted squeeze for me."

When Theresa hung up, the mountains stood black against the

indigo sky. It must have been after midnight in Bucaramanga. Ted's not sleeping much either, she thought. She knew he felt guilty about taking Will to Colombia, about the safety, and about not telling her right away when Will was kidnapped. The brothers had worked on drilling jobs together all their lives and they'd always come back with interesting tales to tell. Will told stories about working six weeks and losing seven weeks' pay in one card game. Ted was still a wild card, but she trusted him. Of all the people who told her how much they cared about her husband, only Ted would put Will's well-being ahead of his own.

Something thudded against her kitchen window. Again. And again. It sounded like someone hitting the glass with mittens on. Tentatively, she looked out the window into the large eyespots of a giant silk moth. The eyespots covered the entire bottom wing of the moth. Each wing was as wide as her hand. Its thick, meaty body thumped against her window, drawn to the light over her sink. She switched the light off and the moth wobbled away. She envied the winged creature. It knew its way through the darkness.

SEVEN

THE AIRPLANE TORE FREE from the clouds and circled Bucaramanga, presenting its passengers with a handsome view of *La Ciudad Bonita*. The city was perched high on a plateau crushed against the Cordillera Oriental, the eastern arm of the Andes Mountains. Nick's eye followed the Rio de Oro from its lush green mountain valley to a knife-edged canyon that outlined the city's western edge. He could see the red tiled roofs of the affluent neighbourhoods rusting into sprawling barrios that crept further up the mountain every year. In the middle of the city stood the tall modern office buildings of Colombia's centre for mining and energy. Nick was struck by its resemblance to Calgary, until the airplane door opened and flooded the fuselage with the promise of a year-round growing season. Nick descended the metal stairway, holding his newspaper and inhaling the fragrances of his adopted country. The warm, moist air sparked a vigour and liveliness that northern countries deadened. Nick Nordstrom was keen to attack the problem awaiting him.

Crosses, gold chains, and strings of beads swung from the taxi's rear-view mirror. An ivory-coloured virgin suctioned to the dash kept a demure eye out for potholes so the driver didn't have to. In his semi-reclined state, the driver sped dangerously close to women walking with bags of groceries, kids playing tag in the street, an old man selling watermelons, young men with wrenches in their back pockets bent over parked cars, and stray dogs without any road sense. As the breeze from the rolled-down window ruffled his hair, Nick marvelled at the driver's luck as he drove, hell-bent and oblivious to everything but his destination. Maybe *all* the taxis in Colombia had ivory virgins.

Suddenly, the driver slammed on his brakes. A motorcycle had rocketed through a stop sign. The girl in the fluttery skirt with her arms around her beau never noticed how close to death she came. The scene carried Nick back twenty-five years, when he and a buddy chose to ride motorcycles from the Darien Gap to Patagonia instead of punching in at the local smelter after high school. The ride implanted a love for everything Latin, especially beautiful, dark-eyed women. And in Colombia, they were all beautiful. He adored the uncomplicated lifestyle of the people who shared their meals and accommodations with two oversexed gringos from *el Norte*. He and Byron sold their bikes for airfare home, but Nick liked to imagine those BMW warhorses still pumping out testosterone across the Argentinean pampas.

Nick stepped out of the taxi in front of his T-Rex of Timmins, Colombia Division office and was assaulted by the smell of burning plastic. He detested how this scourge from the north had invaded the southern hemisphere. Twenty-five years ago, the native insect population could digest everything that humans discarded and turn it into something useful. But now, predator-free and impervious to the elements, plastic garbage accumulated until someone lit a match to it. In this part of the city, matches outnumbered recycling bins.

Nick's "office" was actually a walled-off corner of a warehouse. Before he could wrench the door open, a property guard broke off his conversation with friends to welcome him back home and shake his hand. The T-Rex warehouse overflowed with large and small pieces of drilling equipment, a jumble of new and used machine parts, as well as four high-clearance vehicles, all of which necessitated the guard's watchful eye. Once seated at his desk, Nick cleared a spot and wrote a list of names on a blank sheet of paper. The name at the top was Ted Edwards, the kidnapped man's brother. Nick wanted to know what had happened at the mining camp from a man who wouldn't feed him any bullshit.

— — —

Later that afternoon, Ted arrived at the T-Rex of Timmins headquarters, its address scribbled on the back of a losing lottery ticket. He unfastened his loose ribbon of a seat belt and tipped the driver heavily, happy to have scored a 1981 Chevrolet Classic taxi. Ted loved the big American car — the way it floated through the streets crowded with people, front end high in the air, hood ornament still attached, the entire length of Calle San Miguel.

The door to the T-Rex office hung open. A good three metres away, Ted heard a deep, assertive voice speaking at a North American volume. He waited in the doorway for an invitation to come in. Strips of late afternoon light from a louvered window fell across the floor. A chair stood beside a counter cluttered with maps, papers, full ashtrays, a stained coffee-maker, a photocopier, and a fax machine. The air conditioner was dry and silent. A large desk with a map of Colombia tacked to the wall behind it took up most of the office. Attached to the telephone on the desk was the slight man with the big voice. He rocked back in his chair, nodded in Ted's direction and gestured toward the empty seat. Ted sat down.

"So really, there's nothin' you guys can do?" Nick said. "I remember a situation a few years back where a couple of young kids got themselves in trouble in Brazil. They kidnapped a local businessman in broad daylight. Guilty as hell. With a little bit of public pressure, you guys changed policies and broke rules to get them back to Canada like you had a bad case of election fever. Now you've got the balls to tell me there's nothin' you can do?"

Ted strained to hear the small voice on the other end of the line, then gave up. His attention turned to a curled brown leaf, slightly larger than a jellybean, suspended from one of the window's wooden slats. As he looked more closely, he realized it was not a leaf, but a pupa case, armed with tiny spines. It jiggled and quivered with the energy of life.

"That's good. You talk to him. We're dealin' with a workin' man here — a blue-collar guy that doesn't turn any screws on Bay Street. His only crime is that he's innocent."

The chrysalis shook violently. Ted wondered if it would come unglued. The capsule cracked open at its base and something began to emerge.

"Yeah, I think I do understand. You won't talk to the ARA. Therefore you're tellin' me that you would rather follow official policy and get a dead man back instead of unofficial policy and get a live man back." After a short pause, Nick added, "You did so just say that."

Steadily, the life form unfurled itself from the brown capsule. Ted stared at it. He had never seen this before. A living bit of moist black and yellow glistened on the dusty windowsill.

The tiny voice inside the phone buzzed like an angry bee.

The big voice on the other side of the desk responded, "You bet I understand. You won't do fuck all about anything, and I'm not supposed to get involved. Don't worry about me, Mr. Bernard. I'll just sit here with my thumbs up my ass and wait for your call."

The receiver hit the phone with a force that knocked the old pupa case and the new butterfly onto the floor. Nick's red face turned toward Ted.

"Ted! How the hell are ya?"

They shook hands over top of the trembling telephone.

"That was Bernard at the Canadian embassy in Bogotá. They are so far from the real world over there — it must be the fumes from all the 'Welcome to Crime-Free Colombia' tour buses. Seems I'll just complicate negotiations if I get involved. They've got Bernard right on top of this kidnapping thing. You and me can just sit up at the bar at the Petroleum Club and sip cranberry martinis until Bernard calls. Then we'll just drive Will home. Have you got a station wagon — something suited to hauling long, narrow boxes?"

Ted still hadn't spoken, but he thought Nick wanted him to say something. "Um... no."

Nick continued, "Bernard's gonna talk to a guy that meets regularly with the top anti-kidnapping official in the Colombian government. But that's not gonna happen until next week. You got any idea how many people are fuckin' kidnapped every day in this country? And it's not gonna result in anything until next year. Or maybe when hell freezes over and we're farmin' date palms and butterflies in Tuktoyaktuk. Maybe then."

"What about talking to the ARA?"

"Talkin' to the ARA?" Nick feigned surprise. "Hell no! That might get us somewhere! No, my good man, it has to be government to government, thanks to some trade agreement the Yanks talked us into. You gotta wonder who the terrorists are around here. So much for goddamn official policy."

Ted felt uncomfortable. Nick was supposed to have answers. "What's Blackburn doing about Will's kidnapping?"

Nick snorted in disgust and thumped his hand down hard on the desk. The telephone dinged to attention. "You know where Blackburn is in all this? Lemme show you where Blackburn is, Ted." He picked up the newspaper from the airplane and jammed it in front of him. It was folded open to the business section, page 5. With more than 3,000 kidnappings a year in Colombia, Will's disappearance was not front-page material. Ted barely had time to focus on the dateline — "Vancouver, B.C., Canada (Business Wire)" — before Nick yanked it back.

"Goddamn newspapers around here don't report the news — just beauty queens and post-election bullshit. Any reporter with anything to say got done away with years ago. Anyway, I found this article stuffed onto the bottom of the page here: 'Blackburn Resources International reports that work continues at the Mariposa Gold Silver Project in northeast Colombia.' Bullshit it does..."

He had Ted's attention.

"'Canadian Press reports of kidnapped Blackburn Resources International personnel are in error. One of those reported abducted, William L. Edwards, works for the Colombia Division of T-Rex Drilling of Timmins, Ontario. Blackburn Resources International contracts diamond-drilling services from T-Rex Drilling. Others reported abducted have no relation to Blackburn Resources International whatsoever. Blackburn's Colombian operations are forty-five airline kilometres from Bucaramanga, a city of nearly one million people, near the Venezuelan border. The new president promises a crackdown on abductions of foreign workers in northeast Colombia.' Blah blah blah." Nick stabbed his nicotine-stained finger into the paper. "Here's the good part. 'Blackburn Resources International company spokesperson, E.J. Reyes, says,' and I quote, 'Edwards was not employed by Blackburn Resources International at the time of his abduction.'"

Nick looked directly at Ted and said, "There it is in black and white. You see what's goin' on here?"

Ted figured that Nick would tell him.

"By puttin' this in *El Tiempo*, Blackburn has told the guerrillas that Will is not their man. He's tellin' them, 'Don't come to us for money. *He's not our man.*'" Nick slammed the paper back onto the desk and lit up a cigarette.

"How are the guerrillas going to see this?" Ted asked.

"We're not dealin' with a bunch of hillbillies from below the tracks. I know goddamn well the guerrillas are gonna see this here. That's why Blackburn put it here. They know what's happenin', man. They read newspapers, their Internet is solar-powered, they probably have their own goddamn chatline, and they know how to plug their message to the international press. The Arauca Revolutionary Army is very media-savvy."

Things didn't sit well for Ted. "Blackburn promised us worker protection and Will gets kidnapped from their camp. What gives? Blackburn has to answer for that."

Nick leapt out of his chair and paced the floor. "Yeah, well, Blackburn fucked up. I called them before you busted in and caught me flirtin' with Bernard in Bogotá. All the big players like Blackburn hire their own public relations agencies to cover up the truth when the fit hits the shan. I wish I had a tenth of their spin budget to run my operation on. Hell, even E.J.'s vacation pay would buy me and both my wives a lotta happiness."

His cigarette ash fell on the wooden floor as he paced. "E.J.... we gotta get past that fat bastard and find out some answers. Like worker protection. Why in hell would the ARA come waltzin' into camp and take a worker? And why my driller, for Chrissakes?" Nick's black eyes burned.

Ted didn't respond. He had been raised to admit his mistakes and learn from them. Nick operated his drilling company according to the same code. T-Rex did not budget for public relations.

Nick went on. "E.J. made it quite clear to me. Blackburn Resources International is not gonna get their hands dirty talkin' to guerrillas. He said that if they 'engage in dialogue' — notice how PR people don't talk anymore, they 'engage in dialogue' — they risk being kidnapped themselves."

"Is that true?"

"Sure, there's a risk. But that's just bullshit. Do they want Will outta there or not? What they're really afraid of is the government findin' out they're talkin' to guerrillas. The government and guerrillas have this little war goin' on, so if any company is caught conspirin' with the enemy, that company is gonna lose big. All contracts — wham! Cancelled! That's the last thing Blackburn wants."

"So what about Will?"

"Unfortunately for Will, the ARA's got the wrong fuckin' guy."

— — —

Even before he embarked on discussions with Blackburn and the Canadian embassy in Bogotá, Nick knew he was on his own. He planned to "engage in dialogue" with Canadian Foreign Affairs, but there would be no official help from Canada. Getting Will out of the backcountry would be accomplished unofficially between himself, the ARA, maybe Blackburn, and a hell of a lot of money he didn't have.

Dealing with the Blackburn bastards without killing someone itself presented a challenge. Dealing with the ARA without getting himself killed might be doable. Somehow he had to establish contact, and then the bargaining would begin.

He also needed protection. He'd call Alonso, a big country boy who owed him a favour. Nick had rescued Alonso and his friend from a long weekend at the police station last summer. The friend had been linked to some union shit that Nick did not want to know about. Nick butted his cigarette and started another.

Then there was Ted. Nick wasn't sure what Ted could do, but he could be trusted — and trust was something this beleaguered country held in short supply. It was worth more than all the stolen gold in Spain. He squinted at Ted through the smoke.

"Where are ya?"

"I'm downtown at the Hotel California."

"*Hijo de puta*, man!" Nick thundered. "You need a place where you can sleep at night, not lie awake and wonder which set of footsteps on the back stair is gonna slit your throat. How 'bout Rose's, where I am? Nice little *pension*, clean... what's the matter?"

"Will knows I'm at the Hotel California. If he gets out, he'll look for me there. It's not so bad, you know. The owner and his nephew have put up a new restaurant. The nephew runs it, but Oscar worries about the kid's friends. I told Oscar there's nothing like a fourteen-hour-a-day job to straighten out these young guys. His name is Agustín."

Nick's bushy eyebrows lifted. "Agustín what?"

"Something like Molero-Pérez, or Pérez-Molero."

The blackjack dealer slammed an ace onto the table next to his pair of kings. Nick could not believe the coincidence. Alonso's left-leaning friend was named Agustín Pérez-Molero.

"Okay, Ted. Fine. Just don't sleep on your good ear. Have you contacted Will's family?"

"Yep. I call every day."

"Good man. I'll cover costs for you: room, food, long distance calls. Now. Tell me, from the top, what happened on June 24 at the Mariposa mine site. I gotta know details, man, details."

Before Ted reached the climax of his story, he stopped in mid-sentence. The long-winged butterfly with the pale yellow and black stripes fluttered groggily across the map of Colombia. Both men watched it float past Ted, through the open door, and into the warm Bucaramanga night.

EIGHT

A DISCORDANT MIX OF BIRDSONG IN THE TREES above the camp announced Will's second sunrise in captivity. At ground level, the captives huddled in blankets around the Coleman stove. Will thought a fire might take the chill off the morning, but he also realized that smoke from the fire could give away the camp's location. He washed down his rice and beans with his coffee, and he wondered if he'd drunk the washwater by mistake.

During the night, Will had been wakened by a great urge to relieve himself. He crawled out of the tent to the nearby bushes. He was in mid-piss when he heard a rifle cock behind him, and a female voice demanding, *"Que pretendes hacer?"* He thought it was obvious what he was doing, but the nudge of the gun barrel between his shoulder blades persuaded him to put his hands in the air. The soldier escorted him back to his tent in his wet coveralls. From now on, he would pass on the after-supper coffee.

Following breakfast, the soldiers put away the kitchen, packed up the tents, and loaded the mule. Will rolled the groundsheet tightly and tied it to the outside of his too-small, ill-fitting pack. He ignored the raw spots above his armpits and stood waiting for orders between the same two soldiers as the day before. Despite his blisters, complaining hips, and stiff muscles, he preferred walking to sitting idle. The last two soldiers brushed the ground clear of footprints with a giant palm frond.

The troop set out walking downhill until the path became overgrown and jungle-like. Will found the equatorial forest of Colombia suffocating. The ubiquitous wet greenery seemed to grow back as quickly as the soldiers ahead could slash a passageway through it.

Will could not see daylight above the broad-leaved trees that shaded them. He hadn't known that green came in so many different shades, tones, and textures. Even the air felt green. Mosses and lichens clung to every surface — not only the smooth and sunburned trees, but those girdled by prickly spines. Will noticed hollow trees with flaring buttresses imprisoned by lattices of strangling green. Everywhere he looked, trees, ferns, and ground plants knitted themselves together into one living, flowing garment.

Will thought of Theresa and her houseplants that climbed and bent toward the sunlight in their living room. Some of the plants here looked similar. If she were here, thought Will, she'd enjoy the flowers that bloomed from the trees and the plants that grew on tree branches. He would ask her if "fuchsia" was a colour or a plant. And she would know.

There was no conversation, only the whine and buzz of the attacking insects and the sound of boots ahead and behind. They climbed steadily from the low-lying jungle up into the mountains until they reached an open ridge. It was blanketed by yellow grass which gave them all welcome respite from the insects. The exposed sun burned through Will's cap and made him think of all the ants he'd ever fried under a magnifying glass. With a thirst for freedom, he drank in the panoramic view of sky and landscape. He looked behind to envision the route they had taken to reach the ridge. Where had last night's camp been? He looked ahead to clouded summits and a pair of vultures gliding effortlessly on rising thermals. There was a river below them, a river flowing east to Venezuela.

— — —

They rested in the shade of the forest, a stone's throw from the open ridge. After a lunch of cold rice tortillas, Will, Luis, and José settled in against their packs. Francisco, their guard, sat a few metres away, smoking José's cigarettes. Some of the soldiers had slung their hammocks, some played *fútbol,* and some washed their hair and clothing in the nearby waterfall. The higher altitude and lower humidity gave Will a little more energy than he had the day before.

Luis was perkier as well. He said to Will, "Have you noticed that after two days these soldiers don't look alike anymore? And José knows all the girls' names already."

José remained sullen and uncommunicative.

"What's the name of the big solid girl wearing the Castro cap?" Luis asked.

José's eyes were shaded by his hat, his mouth a thin line. Will was surprised when he answered. "Jenny," he said. "Carolina has the ponytail. The one that hums when she walks is Angela. Zhuri leads the mule."

Will had also been girl-watching, especially the mule girl, Zhuri. She seemed less accustomed to manual labour than the other girls and much too feminine to have been a soldier for long. He would plan his escape for the mule girl's watch.

Luis lit a cigarette. "You don't smoke, Will?"

"Nope. I quit ten years ago and haven't wanted one since."

"How did you do it?"

"My little girl asked me to. She came home from Pat's Day Care one day with her eyes full of tears and said she would miss me when I died from smoking. I had to promise her I wasn't going to die. So I quit." Will shrugged. "I guess something else will have to kill me now."

"I've wanted to quit for years. This may be my best opportunity." Luis thought about it and then added, "As soon as this pack is done."

Will noticed how José eyed Luis' cigarettes. Withdrawal seemed to be making the kid more irritable than usual.

"Where are your cards?" Will asked him.

José looked up, slowly fished the pack out of his shirt pocket, and tossed them over to Will. The worn cards displayed a curvaceous orange-haired woman on stiletto heels glancing over a bare shoulder. The gossamer shawl wound around her was folded double in all the wrong places.

"It's time you two learned a new game." Will dealt each of them seven cards.

— — —

One round of gin rummy later, the captives watched El Capitán and the second-in-command walk past them toward the open ridge. A field radio swung from the second-in-command's hand. He carried earphones and coils of wire in his other hand. The captives continued to watch as the men in charge set up the radio, hunkered down in front of it, and appeared to be making contact with someone, somewhere.

Meanwhile, shouts erupted from the *fútbol* game in the opposite direction. One of the players must have scored. Luis lamented, "Those could be my own boys, Uli and Damien."

Will picked up the discarded queen of spades, laid his cards down, and announced that he was out. They added up their scores as Luis dealt the next hand. Will asked, "Where are your boys now?"

"Technical college in Darmstadt, Germany. One is twenty-four, the other twenty-one. Heidi, my wife, is there too, visiting her parents while I play games with you." Luis' eyes settled on the faraway ridge where the commanders leaned into the radio.

Luis talked about his father, a government official in La Paz, who had pushed him to go to Germany to study metallurgical engineering. When Luis married Heidi two days after graduation, his father was less pleased. "In a forest outside of Darmstadt, we kissed, encircled by friends singing 'All we are saying is give peace a chance.' It was 1970 and Heidi and I decided to stay young and free and in love forever."

When they laid their hands down, José once again had the lowest score, which did not improve his mood. He gathered the cards and dealt while Luis talked. "Heidi was not the aristocratic Latin woman my parents would have chosen for their only son. Instead, she was very blonde and very blue-eyed, and very pregnant. I didn't see the trouble coming when we flew to Bolivia to meet my parents."

The cards waited. José tipped his hat up, appearing to show interest. "The first altercation concerned the length of my hair," Luis said. "Then Father instructed our driver to avoid the demonstration that blocked several of the downtown streets. My blue-suited father knew enough of my blue-jeaned wife's language to argue the threat of anarchy versus the tools of democracy, a heated discussion that quickly fell into accusations of totalitarianism and fascism. Father's familiarity with German gutter talk surprised me and caused Mother to blush." Luis wiped his eyes with the back of his hand and continued, smiling. "Naturally, Mother played referee between the generations until Heidi and I took our so-called 'devilish music' and our 'peace, love, and patchouli oil' back to Europe. But not before Mother had Esmeralda mend the tear in Heidi's jeans."

Will compared the youthful, long-haired Luis in the story to the plump and balding man before him, and thought Luis probably looked more like his father now than his old self.

"Things improved between Mother and Heidi upon our first boy's arrival. Unfortunately, Father's car veered off a mountain road on a state visit to Chile before he ever saw Damien."

The card game resumed. Luis asked, "Have we got time to go to five hundred?"

"Luis, we've got time to go to five hundred million," Will said. He gestured toward Francisco, who had dozed off, his hands slack around his gun. "How did you end up back in South America?"

"Metallurgists are well paid and never out of work in South America. We bought five hectares of Bolivian countryside, built a *Gasthaus*, and Heidi started a butterfly farm. The German travellers enjoy the butterflies almost as much as the beer. Heidi makes the best *Schwarzwälder Kirschtorte* in all of Bolivia, which explains why I carry all these extra kilos." Luis grabbed his belly for emphasis.

Will complimented the two men on their cardplaying, even though he was first to reach five hundred again. Luis congratulated him and asked if they should start another game. Will shrugged as if to say what else is there to do, and asked how he and José ended up in his jeep two days ago.

"*Canadienses creídos!*" José blurted out in disgust. "You think you're so good."

"What the hell?" Will looked over at José.

José jumped at the bait, ready for a fight. "If your Canadian companies don't want to play by the house rules, then don't play. Luis and I are collateral damage because you *Canadienses creídos* want it all your way — you take what you want and never pay the full price. I'm sick and tired of eating shit and being led around like a fucking mule."

So that was the bug the kid had up his ass: José held Will responsible for his capture. Will stifled a rude response. He was not about to get into an argument in defense of Canadian mining companies with José. He suggested they get on with the game.

"Forget it. I quit." José stood up. Francisco woke suddenly and tightened the grip on his rifle.

"Where in the hell do you think you're going? We're all in this together." Luis told José to sit down, then gathered the cards and shuffled. He and Will knew it was important to keep José away from the soldiers. One unruly captive could result in punishment for all three of them. "Explain the Rio de Oro project to Will."

José squatted down and said acidly in Will's direction, "We're just cleaning up your fucking mess."

The hair on Will's arms prickled.

Luis attempted to restore the peace. "These multinational mining companies have to try harder to reduce their impacts on the environment — "

"Especially you *Canadienses imperialistas*," José interjected. "You bring your money and your machines that have no respect for the earth and you take our gold and throw glass beads at the people. What do we get out of it?"

"We come down here and we give guys like you jobs," Will said.

"Everybody just calm down. We don't need people laying blame," said Luis. "These problems are worldwide. We need to build environmental protection, labour laws, and human rights into our trade agreements. Communication needs to be improved between all the stakeholders, and we all have to sit around the same table. It's the only way we can balance quality of life with the bottom line."

Luis turned to Will. "José and I were hired by a Canadian environmental group in partnership with the German government. People on the Rio de Oro have used mercury to separate precious metals from river sand for generations. There isn't anything out there that can attract gold like mercury — and it forms such a beautiful, glittering amalgam."

"Until they burn off the mercury," José said. All three of the men knew the toxic effects of mercury vapour. "When you can't sell your restricted or banned substances in North America, you dump them down here."

Luis agreed that mercury was too cheap, too plentiful, and too available. He and José had witnessed the memory loss and inattentiveness in the rural people along the river firsthand. When they analyzed the fish, the main staple of the local diet, they found elevated levels of the metal. Mercury spilled into the river every day. Kids sifted it through their fingers; they made the metal flow and form beads in the palms of their hands. The local people, many of them indigenous, chose to ignore the damaging effects. Luis looked to José for confirmation.

"The Rio de Oro project is an example of what I was talking about," Luis said. "With this new method developed by the environmental group, and with the necessary German marks, we can show the people how to extract the gold from the sediment without the use of mercury at no extra cost. The mining companies want to see success before they adopt the idea. The only negative aspect of the project is this hostage-taking situation we find ourselves in. We left the work unfinished."

"Shitload of good we're doing here," added José.

El Capitán and the second-in-command reappeared and walked past the three men without so much as acknowledging them. Their nonchalance bothered Will. He pointed to their radio and asked, "What kind of pizza did you order?"

El Capitán's frown deepened. Will grinned. The commander then gave the order for everyone to pack up and move out.

— — —

A warm afternoon rain fell from saturated clouds. It coated everything as neatly as a North American supermarket sprinkler mists its produce section. Water dripped from every leaf, every vine, every stem, every flower, and every green and growing thing. When the sun emerged, Will felt as if they were hiking through a greenhouse, squeezed by plants that seemed to breathe.

Before dark, they set up camp. The soldiers on supper duty opened a tin of sardines and divided it by fifteen, adding what Will called a "hearty meat component" to the main course of rice and beans.

Under the "big top," Will sported his pajamas and grinned at his tentmates. Luis, the man in the middle, chuckled. José ignored him, faced the tent wall, and fell asleep.

Outside the tent, Will and Luis could hear the commanders and soldiers discuss the "global ravages of capitalism and the imminent revolution" after which "the glorious movement would triumph over Yankee imperialism." Will dubbed it *la hora cultural*, or culture hour. In order to block out the sound of the lesson, Luis would talk about his polo pony and the matches they played, and Will would recount hunting adventures from his past. He remembered the travelling storytellers who entertained his family when he was a boy, in the time before television and computers. But it wasn't until now that he understood the value of the storyteller. Stories from another time and another place had an analgesic effect, and therefore were of great value. More valuable, in fact, than all the butterflies, beer, and *Schwarzwälder Kirschtorte* in Bolivia.

NINE

ON MONDAY AFTERNOON, Theresa hung out the laundry and cleaned house. If the telephone rang, she would not hear it over the sound of the vacuum cleaner. Will's three sisters and their husbands left early in the morning — Millie and Cameron went west, June and Jackson went north, and Mary and Andy went east.

A weekend with Will's sisters had taught Theresa more things about her husband than she had learned in fourteen years of marriage. She hadn't known that Will had spent three years in Grade One because he needed glasses; all she knew was that he'd quit school at age fifteen. The teacher had asked the class to sing. Will defied her by refusing to sing or whistle, so he was asked to leave. It made sense to Theresa now. He was almost a man in a class of twelve-year-old kids — no wonder he wouldn't sing. Theresa had always blamed the good-paying jobs at the mine that were available to anyone who could walk over and ask for one.

The sisters recalled several stunts Will and Ted had pulled as boys. Unfortunately, they paid dearly for their last one. When they were caught breaking into a local pool hall to raid the candy counter, the boys were sentenced to two years in reform school. The experience had cemented their closeness and taught them how to stand up for themselves. Theresa hoped Michael didn't get any ideas about emulating his father.

Ted phoned every night and talked to Theresa and each of his sisters more than he had in a lifetime. It was good for him to know he had support from the family and that no one blamed him for Will's situation. He seemed to need that.

Everyone had laughed when Uncle Bud got a little tipsy and stepped in the dog dish, splattering dog food all over Auntie June's Velcro running shoes. As a result, old Snorty had the hots for June all weekend — but only when she strapped on her running shoes. Auntie Millie lent Kelly a sympathetic ear. Mary took command of the kitchen and cooked as if she expected a drilling crew for supper. Bud made sure the liquid refreshments never ran dry. Will's presence drifted around the table like smoke as they played cards until dawn. Conversations swirled about Calgary's land-greedy subdivisions, traffic congestion in the lower mainland, the diamond boom in Yellowknife, and how much money each could afford to help buy Will's freedom. Theresa could detect traces of Will in each of his sisters — in their smiles, the shape of their hands, the way they said certain phrases and words, the slope of their shoulders — commonalities that gave her moments of padded sadness.

What the heck? Her weeping fig tree in the corner of the living room looked like a skeleton. Dry, rumpled leaves huddled around its base. Theresa stuck her fingers into its big Mexican pot — bone dry. She looked around; all of her houseplants were suffering from neglect. As she hustled to the sink for a pitcher of water, she thought of Millie's premonition.

"I felt that we were about to receive good news about Will," Millie had said. "The closer we came to Monarch Valley, the stronger the feeling grew." That night when Ted called from Colombia, he said he had good news. All eyes turned to Millie. She responded with Will's wide grin. The good news, Ted explained, was that Will's jacket was missing from the warehouse. If the guerrillas planned to kill him, they would not have taken his jacket. The news put to rest the dark possibility no one dared speak out loud.

Theresa asked Ted if anyone had heard from the guerrillas yet.

"No," Ted said, "they haven't contacted anyone yet. I hear this is normal. The longer they wait, the more worried the family gets. The more worried we get, the more pressure we apply, and more money comes through. They don't give out any information too soon — it's only been ten days." Uncle Bud christened it the "sweat factor."

Theresa couldn't believe it had only been ten days.

— — —

When Theresa first met Will, she was barely twenty years old and mildly intrigued by his forty-one years of accumulated bad habits. While at business college, she had signed up as "chief cook and bottle-washer" for a drilling camp outside of Troy in northwest British Columbia. She thought about those wasted secretarial skills whenever she kneaded the 5:30 AM dough, peeled the wheelbarrows of potatoes, broiled the moose-sized steaks, fried the tear-stained onions, drove the boat across Graveyard Lake for groceries, and ordered the men to take their boots off the table. The drillers even learned to remove their hats when they sat at her tables, which were graced with wild-flowers and set with more than one fork. She blushed when the hand-some, dark-haired foreman with the wide grin called her "Cookie."

Several company executives in Canadian mining owed their edu-cation in the drilling business to Will Edwards. Will had chosen to remain on the crew when many of the men he trained washed the drill mud from their hands and entered the office. Will preferred physical labour to the mental stress that came with a desk job. He didn't own a tie and he never wanted to have to buy one.

Will thought Theresa looked fabulous. When she glanced at him with her big, brown eyes, he felt twenty years younger. Warm countries teemed with women with enticing eyes, but Theresa's promised honesty and kindness. And she liked to laugh — all the way down those long legs to her toes. Aside from her physical appearance, he admired her ability to handle a hungry drilling crew.

Theresa had been warned about drilling crew foremen — how wives could never compete with the adventurous allure of their work. When she listened to Will's stories about nights in a Mendoza jail cell, frozen hose lines in the Arctic, cathouses in El Salvador, and winning lottery tickets in Panama, she could not picture the man in a domestic setting. He smoked too much, drank too much, gambled too much, got in trouble too much — and the thought of all those foreign-born parasites made her shudder. She wiped the long oil-cloth-covered tables clean as the smell of baking bread wafted from the camp kitchen window into the drilling field.

Sometimes Will thought about a home life, but his job required his full attention. He could concentrate much better if he didn't have to smell that fresh bread. Besides, he'd never met the right woman. As he tested the strength of the tailing pond wall, he wondered if Theresa liked him. Maybe, as the song on the radio at the time suggested, it was time for a cool change.

Theresa often asked Will if it was her or her cooking that he fell in love with.

— — —

The new furniture that had stacked up in the Copper Crescent driveway obscured the two-metre-high pink flamingo with the "just married" sign around its neck. Theresa had looked at the familiar mountain scenery behind her new house. Nestled between two mountain ranges, Monarch Valley had been an idyllic place to grow up. Not until the final years of high school did Theresa feel the shift from homey security to smothering imprisonment. She joined the migration of young people drawn to the city beyond the protection/confinement of the Skimmerhorn Range. Upon her return as a married woman, the endearing closeness of the small town hugged her and frightened her at the same time. Would her new husband feel the embrace, or would he feel like a butterfly pinned to a corkboard?

Theresa poured a second jug of water down the throat of the big Mexican pot. The fig tree was a living reminder of their island honeymoon in Curaçao. Between rounds of sexual exploration, she and Will golfed at a resort ringed with hedges of perfumed oleander, pink against a blue ocean vista. After a suicidal slice to the right, Theresa searched the rough in vain for her lost ball. Instead, she found an interesting variety of wild houseplants. A dollhouse-sized plant snuggled in the arms of another tree fascinated her. It would make a perfect bonsai. She plucked it out, wrapped it in a wet handkerchief, secured it in the pocket of her golf bag, and then forgot about it until she got home.

Maybe these same plants surrounded Will right now as she watered them. Then she laughed, thinking how odd it would be if Will actually noticed that.

TEN

WILL WAS ADJUSTING to his new nomadic lifestyle. The guerrillas moved camp every day as if they were being watched. Each morning, scouts were dispatched to seek out possible paramilitary activity and establish the evening camp prior to the troop's arrival. If the guerrilla group had to cross open fields or pass near settlements, they would often travel at night to avoid detection.

In the dark, Will felt vulnerable and awkward. His sixty-year-old eyes could not always make out what his youthful captors saw. He often stumbled on the uneven ground, catching himself before he fell with the walking stick that Fidel had carved for him. The staff was solid and made from wood as hard as granite. Earlier in the week, Will had complimented the young soldier on the workmanship of the new handle on the latrine shovel. A few days later, the hardwood staff had appeared outside his tent.

In the dark, Will had to feel for the dips and rocks on the trail with his staff and his feet. The exercise reminded him of an excursion his daughter had participated in with the Girl Guides last summer. The Guides called it "Night Trek," and it was Kelly's first event with the group. Will remembered squinting into the setting sun as he drove his daughter and her friend to Azure Creek Park for the event. Their excitement was contagious and their conversation nonstop.

"Who did Illana and Marina join up with?" Kelly asked.

"I think Cora and Stephanie." Kat answered. "What if we lose the trail — or worse, what if *we* get lost?"

"Ohmigod!" Kelly said. "Don't even think about it! Are there any bears out here, Dad?" Before Will could answer, she went on: "I need some new hiking shoes — these are definitely too small. I'll probably get blisters. I saw some cool blue ones in McDermott's...."

"Oh yeah, I saw those too. I like the mirrors on the laces. Did you see those new tankini tops?"

When do these girls breathe? he wondered.

Dusk had settled over the park by the time they arrived. Kelly and Kat rushed over to the bonfire where the Girl Guides had gathered. Will could see that a great deal of organization, parent participation, and girlish gutsiness had contributed to the event's success. Kim, the Guide leader, stoked a blaze that promised to outlive the night. Surrounded by this gaggle of girls and their mothers, Will felt very male and hugely outnumbered. It was, he admitted, a pleasant change from the drilling world.

The girls were required to hike five kilometres in the dark to earn their Night Trek designation. The Azure Creek trail dodged around a wetland and climbed through forest to a waterfall before circling back. At each kilometre, two parents manned a station connected to Kim via walkie-talkie. Will knew Kelly was afraid; nevertheless, she followed her flashlight beam into the dead of night, no matter what lurked, loomed, skulked, or slithered out there.

Will remembered his own night treks under the northern lights. Back then, a night trek was simply how you got from point A to point B after the sun went down, and he couldn't recall getting any badges for it.

"Have fun," said Kim as she sent out a group of four girls every thirty minutes. "It's important to stay together as a group and check in at each station. Remember to talk to each other all the time." That last reminder hardly seemed necessary, Will remarked to himself.

Fortified by thermoses of hot tea, Will and Vivian Ma waited at Station Number Three for the groups to check in. They heard the girls long before they arrived. They described encounters with frogs as big as teachers' desks, and complained about the shortage of bathrooms along the trail. Despite the exaggerations, Will admired the girls for braving the great unlit unknown, a world far from the shining comforts of the Monarch Valley Mall. As he drove home into the rising sun, the silence from the back seat told its own story.

— — —

At the midnight break, the soldiers and captives maintained their order as they sat down on the trail and rested against the mountain. A comfortable warmth seeped into Will's tired back from the rock, which had faced the afternoon sun. Hungry, dark clouds sniffed at the half moon and then scuttled away. Will spoke quietly to his guard. "How long have you been with the ARA, Frank?"

"Almost two years."

The air tasted cool and humid and carried the smell of grass. Insects whirred loudly throughout their conversation. In the moonlight, Will noticed Francisco's slim build — he did not yet occupy a man's body. "Are you from around here?"

"Sí, Señor. Me, Alejandro, Fidel, Juan, and Jesús live in the area. I'm about a day's walk from my village."

Will thought of his own son's boyhood jammed with Saturday morning cartoons, hockey, baseball, and videogames. Francisco didn't play videogames — he lived them. Will had seen Francisco assemble an AK-47 with more speed and efficiency than he could put a sentence together. Francisco could read the clouds, the stars, and the tracks on the trail, but he could not read the instructions on the Coleman stove. He could probably build a shelter and create fire from the same materials his ancestors had used, but Will doubted his knowledge of history reached beyond his grandfather's memory.

"You guys ever go to school?"

"I went to the school in my village until I got big enough to cut the cane. I never did that good at school, not like my little sister. She wants to be the teacher some day. Alejandro and me joined the ARA as soon as we could. This is a holiday — just like Disneyland in America." Francisco's grin lit up the darkness.

"Disneyland, eh?" Will laughed.

"Oh yeah, *Señor Eduardo.* I set up tents. I watch you. I get food every day. That's not so hard. And the ARA is a good teacher." Francisco told Will about his first assignment, when he had to track an invasive group of paramilitaries. He watched their every move, crawling on his stomach in the grass for two days without food, water, or toilet facilities.

"When I got back and reported in, they gave me this." Francisco held up his AK-47 with a new father's pride.

Will agreed. It was a nice rifle. He thought about Francisco's story. What could he learn in school that would give him the skills he needed to survive in his world, in his modern-day Colombia?

— — —

By the end of their break, the clouds had grown and devoured the moon. Forced to trust his ears more than his eyes, Will followed the sound of the invisible soldier's footsteps on the rocky trail ahead of him. At a sharp bend, his head hit an overhanging wall of rock. He crumpled, not knowing what hit him, and rolled off the trail down an embankment. How far to the bottom? A metre, or a drop as deep as the Nahanni River Canyon? His feet pedalled the air as he clambered for a toehold. He grasped at plants that pulled out of the ground and refused to hold him. As he slid further down into the unknown, he heard Francisco call, "*Señor Eduardo!*"

A sinewy arm stretched out toward him. With only one hand in contact with solid ground, Will swung and took the arm in a viselike hold. He then braced his feet against the crumbling slope. Will felt the young soldier's strength flow through his hand and knew that Francisco would not let him fall. Will clawed his way upward until both feet stood squarely on the trail.

Then he froze. "My glasses!" He dropped to his knees and patted the ground. Without his glasses, he could kiss any chance of escape to Venezuela goodbye. An agonizing minute went by until Francisco, also on his knees, exclaimed, "Aha! *Señor Eduardo*, is this what we look for?"

Will grabbed his glasses from Francisco. Cautiously, he straightened the badly bent frame and cleaned the lenses on his shirt. His hands shook and his heart raced. Once his glasses were safely on his nose, Francisco returned his wooden staff.

"*Señor Eduardo*, when you are from *el Norte*, you think you can blast through walls of rock," he said. "But here, you have to learn patience. You must go around walls like a good Colombian. It is a longer journey, but not so hard."

Will spoke to the white teeth. "Thanks, Frank. I'll try and remember that. Without my glasses, you would have had to lead me around like the girl leads the mule." As he wiped his glasses on his shirt one more time, Will dared to ask the soldier a favour. "I need to get something from my pack."

Francisco waited with his rifle relaxed in the crook of his arm. Will pulled a couple of long white strips from his roll of toilet paper. "If these hang from your pack when you walk ahead of me, I'll be able to keep up."

Francisco agreed. He attached the toilet paper strips to his pack, and Will followed less blindly through the night, holding onto the memory of his brave thirteen-year-old daughter.

ELEVEN

BLOATED GARBAGE BAGS SWELLED to near-bursting in the heat as Agustín and Mercedes stood over the discarded body at *El Carrasco,* the Bucaramanga landfill on the edge of the city. The sight sickened them. They didn't have to turn the figure face up to confirm its identity. Agustín knelt down, brushed the flies away momentarily, and covered what remained of the head with his handkerchief. He wept as he untied his friend's hands, and tried to straighten his stiffened fingers. Mercedes prayed through her handkerchief, which she held over her nose.

Heaps of putrefying waste had metastasized from horizon to horizon. Gulls rose above shimmering waves of heat, screaming at each other over stolen trinkets. The poorest of the poor — the physically handicapped, the mentally ill, the abused, the abandoned mothers with too many children — lived within the dirty and dangerous confines of the city dump. Gleaning food, bottles, rags, metal, and anything unbroken from the seven hundred tons of garbage that arrived each day, they sold their finds to buyers who arrived in the late afternoon. The garbage pickers called the area *Plaza del Gobierno*. This also was the place where the Secret Service deposited its politically unclean bodies. Agustín thanked the reeking man named Zorro who had led them there, and gave him a handful of pesos to cover the body and keep the carrion-eaters away. Lorca and Jorge would be sent to retrieve it after the buyers were gone. Agustín and Mercedes wrapped their arms around each other and retraced their steps through the refuse and around the cellophane-choked slime pools. An annoyed murder of crows flapped out of their way as a cathedral bell tolled in the background.

It wasn't the first dead body Agustín had seen — just the first one he'd known. Sebastian De Coste had taught political science at the University of Bucaramanga. Like many labour organizers before him, De Coste did not live to see old age — his death appeared to be another extrajudicial execution of a trade unionist. Judging by the bruises on his body, he'd been beaten and probably made to walk to his gravesite before dawn this morning. At least his murderers had not dressed him in guerrilla fatigues to fake a combat killing. Agustín wondered if Sebastian felt the bullet explode in his head.

He and Sebastian had distributed petitions on campus in support of an organic coffee grower whose success had made him a target. The police had arrested the grower, Hermano García, for tax evasion, but the ruse was thin. Rumours of García's torture in prison circulated widely. Through educated people like De Coste, the union of organic coffee growers supplied an increasing number of North American coffee buyers. García called his business plan "fair trade" as opposed to "free trade," and his funding came indirectly from the Arauca Revolutionary Army.

The unjust treatment of García led Agustín down the fiery path of trade unionism, anti-globalization, government corruption, and eventually to the ARA itself. Agustín's picture beside *"Liberen a García"* banners appeared in student newspapers, the first publications in the country to go online. When he joined the movement, he was told he was one of many urban messengers throughout the city. He received his own personal Pentium II computer, the latest model in the United States and unavailable in Bucaramanga retail stores. Excited by the speed, power, and uncensored freedom of the new medium, Agustín launched García's speeches into cyberspace, convinced that home computers could succeed where assault rifles could not.

However, the newly paved "information highway" was not exclusive to the university crowd, and its users were often too idealistic to show concern for security. It's how Nick Nordstrom found the background information on Agustín, and it's how factions unfriendly towards trade unions found Sebastian De Coste.

When Agustín left home to attend the University of Bucaramanga, his parents, who were not wealthy, looked to education to provide a higher standard of living for their son, and a haven from violence. Throughout the country, poverty and its attendant violence remained appallingly common. Agustín's mother, Marie-Elena Pérez, and his father, Raimon Molero, were born in the early 1950s, and had never known life without war. As children, they survived the ten-year period known as *La Violencia*, during which an estimated 300,000 Colombians died. Following *La Violencia*, the promised "decade of hope" failed to materialize. The party of the left transmogrified into the party of the right; liberal and free became corrupt and militarized. The Colombian army gained more power, aided by foreign countries and multinational companies with interests in Colombia, the gateway to South America. Guerrilla groups sprouted up in retaliation to the injustices. *La Violencia* continued into the next decade with more mass arrests, intimidation, murder, torture, disappearances, and routine assassinations. Corruption flourished. Drugs proliferated. As more arms were bought and sold, more people could kill and die for peace. And in the process, peace became less and less attainable for ordinary Colombians like Marie-Elena and Raimon.

Agustín could not feign "work as usual" when he returned from El Carrasco. Even after scouring his body from head to toe, washing his hair, and discarding his clothing, he remained convinced that his patrons could smell the stench of death upon him. He washed his hands until they became red and chapped. Mercedes told him she would take the late bus back to Bogotá so she could "help in the kitchen" until closing time. She could tell he needed her strength.

It was barely dark when Agustín switched off the neon sign that spelled out "Sebastian's" — a tribute to his younger brother. There was a burst of electricity and then nothing. Like a bullet crashing through a skull into soft brain tissue. The name "Sebastian's" now assumed new meaning: political resistance was not without its sacrifice. In the shadow of the lifeless sign, Agustín declared that he would not renew his commitment with the ARA. He was getting in too deep, and he didn't like hiding his involvement from Uncle Oscar while operating out of the Hotel California. After all, his Uncle Oscar was a pretty cool guy.

Oscar was really Agustín's mother's uncle, but he didn't want Agustín to call him "great" until he earned the title. At a youthful seventy-three, Oscar welcomed Marie-Elena and Raimon's son to the Hotel California. The boy had a healthy work ethic, and to Oscar, he embodied the spirit of youth — energetic, educated, and hopeful, a model for a country plagued with a violent past and insecure present. With Oscar's blessing (as well as his money), Agustín transformed the old cantina into a respectable restaurant. Agustín appreciated his great-uncle's support and the opportunity to put the lessons he'd learned at his hotel and restaurant management program into practice. Over the course of two years, they redesigned the kitchen from floor to ceiling and installed new sinks, counters, and appliances. They even splurged on a secondhand espresso machine. Their pride and joy, however, was the built-in brick parrilla, a wood-fired grill commonly used in Argentina for cooking large chunks of meat. White curtains fluttered behind planters of palm trees, hibiscus, and butterfly bushes. Agustín managed the restaurant, established a varied menu, hired staff, shopped, and cooked while Oscar beamed. The ripples of renewal could be felt throughout the entire *ciudad vieja* as people returned to the Hotel California.

"We'll be together
With a roof right over our heads
We'll share the shelter
Of my single bed."

Agustín sang along with Bob Marley, slightly off-key. He traced a finger down Mercedes' bare backbone as he coaxed her awake. When he got to the very bottom vertebra, she squirmed, and he walked his fingers all the way back to the top of her neck. Then he began to massage her, slowly and knowingly, down, down, down, to the rhythm of the song easing out of the computer speakers. He had wired a CD burner into his computer — revolutionary technology for 1998 in more ways than one — and could copy any music he wanted.

Agustín would be allowed to keep his Pentium II even after the ARA assigned another messenger to a different neighbourhood. At present, email messages could not be traced back to the Hotel California, although Uncle Oscar often quizzed him about his costly late-night telephone calls.

"Is this love,
Is this love,
Is this love,
That I'm feelin?"

With every "love" he tapped on Mercedes' back while singing into her gardenia-scented hair.

"I think it's the springs in this bed that I'm feelin'," Mercedes mumbled into the pillow as she moved closer to Agustín, almost pushing him onto the floor. He held onto her shoulder to maintain his space on the worn mattress, which gave him the opportunity to place a kiss on the warm spot at the base of her long, smooth neck.

"Yes, I know,
Yes, I know,
Yes, I know, now.
Ever-y day and ever-y night..."

"Do you believe that someday people will get all their news from the Internet instead of the newspaper?" Mercedes asked, now fully awake and aware that time had passed. She needed to catch a bus, and if she left within the next thirty minutes, she might make it back to the capital tonight. Of course, she had explained all that to Agustín four CDs ago, before she had kissed his body all over. She swung her legs around him and put her feet on the scattered pages of *El Tiempo*. She balled up Section B and threw the wad at him.

He caught the crumpled paper. "The Internet is the future," he said. "Newspapers will go the same way as chain belts and button-up jeans. And maybe that's a good thing — they get between a guy and his naked girlfriend and cause bad things to happen." He tossed the ball of paper back and lunged toward her. She rolled away from him and picked through the pile of clothing on the floor.

"But wait!" Agustín added. "I could be mistaken! Newspapers like *El Semanario de Pamplona* will still be very useful if you have a new puppy."

"You shouldn't trash your mother's newspaper." She glared at him and began buttoning her blouse.

"Never in twenty years has she stepped beyond the government gag to print the truth."

"Well, she didn't want to end up like Sebastian De Coste. She had three children. She couldn't put her family in danger. Journalists are just as vulnerable as trade unionists around here." Mercedes zipped up her fashionable, form-fitting jeans.

"When I told her she lived a lie, she said that she learned her lesson early — that silence is the only way to survive Colombia."

"In what way?"

"As senior editor, Mother didn't believe that survivors of violent times needed to know which drug cartel financed the winning *fútbol* team, which multinational clear-cut the Baltimore oriole's winter habitat. People didn't need to wonder why so many of us risk everything to leave this country. Every week she printed *El Presidente's* promises of peace and prosperity. She didn't write about kidnappings, homicides, a paralyzed judicial system, or decades of insurgency. Colombians didn't want to read about it, and her job was to write stuff that would sell papers."

"Exactly. She had her reasons for doing what she did. Your parents put you through university, and they will do the same for your sister, if she gets her head together. Are you going to escort me to the bus depot in your birthday suit? I really have to go. Now."

"Yes, but if the media is not objective, whose job is it to hold up the mirror so that we can judge ourselves? People have to know what's happening in their own country — how can you have a democratic society if everything is held in secret? If people who take pictures are exiled?" He threw on a rumpled T-shirt and jeans, tied his shoulder-length hair behind him, grabbed his wallet and keys, and followed Mercedes out the door.

"Don't forget," she said, "your mother was a radical young woman when she lived in Cartagena, and it almost cost her her life. Things have to change — but slowly. These are dangerous times."

"They've always been dangerous times," Agustín said, thinking back to when Uncle Oscar told Agustín about his mother. Oscar said that he'd been watching Simon and Garfunkel's Central Park concert on TV the night Marie-Elena knocked on his door at the Hotel California.

His niece had worked for *La Prensa Libre de Cartagena*. One day, the newspaper office received an ominous burial wreath. All the journalists received invitations to their own funerals. *La Prensa* defied the threat and continued to write their editorials even after all the other newspapers had been silenced. The next night, the office's front window was sprayed with gunfire, and the editor died shielding Marie-Elena from the bullets. Alone, afraid, and on the run from people she could not identify, Marie-Elena fled Cartegena. When she tried to leave the country by boat, the militia stole her passport; as a journalist, she was considered a "person of suspicion."

Oscar promised to help her find the means to cross the border at Venezuela. But first, he insisted, she should have the glass fragments removed from her hands and knees. He knew a good medical man close by. With silver tweezers and a steady hand, Raimon Molero plucked out the painful shards at a back-alley *farmacia*. He proposed to Marie-Elena six months later, and they began a new life together in the small city of Pamplona, an hour's drive from Bucaramanga. Only in each other's arms could they find the peace their country could not deliver. When Agustín relayed this story to Mercedes, she too was touched. His parents never talked much about their past.

"Someday I'll own a bigger bed, and then you will stay." Agustín locked the door of his room, two doors down from Ted Edwards' room. Mercedes's high-heeled boots clicked rapidly down the tiled stairway ahead of him.

"Someday, when you have your own five-star hotel and restaurant with a view of the ocean, and can hire people to wash dishes instead of me, then I'll come and stay."

They raced across the quiet street in front of the Hotel California and ran all the way to the downtown bus depot.

TWELVE

THE SOLDIERS FELT IT before they heard it. A quick and steady rhythm. Like a nervous drumbeat. Or a fearful heartbeat. Coming closer.

Francisco threw a camouflage blanket at Will and motioned him to get down and cover up. Then he dissolved into the landscape along with the other soldiers and captives. From beneath the blanket, Will heard ammunition clips click into place. The release of safeties. Then the sound of helicopters.

Suddenly, El Capitán's voice erupted. *"Esas botas! Cubranle las botas al cautivo!"*

Will didn't notice that when he crouched down on his elbows and knees, he had left his feet uncovered. His yellow boots flashed like gold nuggets in a pan of washed gravel. Suddenly, someone jerked at his blanket and tucked it under his feet. Seconds later, the air filled with the sound of a helicopter. So loud, so close. Then another. Two helicopters directly above him... *chop... chop... chop...*. Will pictured the pilots looking down. Were they looking for him? Will imagined each guerrilla soldier pressed against a tree. Motionless. Eyes looking up. Buried alive under slabs of air chopped from the sky *...chop... chop ... chop....*

Crouched uncomfortably in a child's position, Will's foot began to cramp. Ugh! If only he could stretch his leg out... *chop...chop... chop...* But then his boot would be uncovered. His yellow boots had been a constant affront to the commander and wearing them gave Will a feeling of defiance. The helicopter pilots would see the movement of the yellow boot. For the first time since his abduction, Will controlled his future. And the future of his captors. He gritted his teeth beneath his blanket. The cramp in his foot spread into his calf muscle. Must... not... move. *...chop... chop...chop...*

But what if he *did* move? Instant relief. And the power to put an end to his captivity. If he alerted the pilots, would he regain his previous life? Or would El Capitán have him shot before he could be rescued? Will felt the man's eyes upon him — steel-grey eyes drilling through the blanket into his back. The commander was forced to trust his captive.

Will's breath fogged his glasses. His leg was one giant, painful spasm. The sound of the helicopters grew fainter. From beneath his blanket he envisioned two American-made scouting helicopters shrinking ... shrinking ... shrinking ... until they became thudding dots on a blue sky beyond the ridge — the same ridge he would soon run along, the one where he would stretch his legs far beyond the limits of muscle and bone. All the way to freedom.

THIRTEEN

A WAR RAGES EVERY SUMMER IN MONARCH VALLEY. The enemy bores through and chews up the valley's fruit and vegetable crops. The people of the agricultural valley rally against the caterpillars with a chemical arsenal. Every year the people claim to win the battle of the orchard, the battle of the garden, and the battle of the field. But in the end, the caterpillars win the war.

Theresa felt defeated. She'd never had a problem remaining positive before. She avoided newspapers and television news because she couldn't manage the world's misfortunes on top of her own. Black crosses marked the July days on the kitchen calendar hanging by the telephone. The telephone — she hated being tied to the damned thing, but she didn't want to hear Will's last words on an answering machine. Every day family and friends called. The conversations were short, but the minutes added up. Whenever the telephone stole her attention, the kids squabbled.

The tabloids seemed to have a nose for misery. Publications she'd never heard of "discovered" her in the same way Native Americans found themselves discovered in 1492. She told them she had no news, even when they persisted. What would they write, she wondered? "Family of captured man waited today/yesterday/the day before. They will wait again tomorrow." The only action was the heartache cannibalizing her and her family. And that made lousy headlines.

Foreign Affairs called twice a week. The department seemed to attract people incapable of relating to someone with a kidnapped husband or father. The last time they called, Michael threw a tantrum. With the phone still pressed to her ear, Theresa sent him to his room. "We never go anywhere!" he sobbed. "You're always on the phone!" With the other ear, she heard James Litchfield admonish her for Nick's actions — he should not take matters into his own hands, he said; he should not talk to the guerrillas. She didn't understand why Litchfield didn't talk to Nick himself. The official reminded her that any kind of comment to, or interaction with the media, even over the Internet, could jeopardize the detainee. "That's all we can tell you," Litchfield would conclude, as if Foreign Affairs knew something she didn't. She swore she heard the phone click a second time after he hung up.

Every second night, either Ted or Nick called from Colombia. Even though they still had no word from the guerrillas, Theresa liked to hear Nick's voice. He assured her the guerrillas didn't deprive or torture their prisoners, and that Will was probably still alive. Exuding confidence, Nick repeated that he knew how things worked in Colombia. She did not forward Litchfield's message to him. Theresa felt that if anything could be done, Nick would do it — guns ablaze. Unlike Foreign Affairs, Nick promised to bring Will home.

The altercation with Kelly started after Nick's call.

"No, you can't go to a party up the lake tonight."

"It's just a bunch of us girls at Armstrong's cabin. It's not like a Stump Flats bush party."

"I said *no*."

"Why can't I go? We never go anywhere! It's been over a month, and like, nothing's happened. Everything's so *fucking* stupid!"

Theresa retreated outside to the garden. Was every Friday night going to be a battle? Damn it all, the kids were right — they never went anywhere. Theresa missed Will. He had more patience with Kelly, and when he said no, she actually listened. She prayed his captors wouldn't hurt him. She remembered movies about prisoners of war unable to cope with normal life. Would Will be scarred, physically, emotionally, when he got home? *If* he got home?

Tears fell between the rows of carrots as she yanked out handfuls of weeds. Where did all this green stuff come from? She and Will planted this garden just before he left for Colombia. How could stinkweed grow so fast?

She turned her back on the carrots and looked at her roses, fuzzy with aphids sucking the life out of them. Where was that spray bottle of insecticidal soap the kids gave her for Mother's Day? It was their last celebration together as a family. She found an old Kleenex in her pocket and blew her nose.

A yellow Miata convertible squealed around the crescent and stopped defiantly in front of Theresa and her infested roses. Will had ribbed Dionne about buying a car based on its colour performance. Dionne told him not to be so cheeky. She claimed that she bought it for safety reasons — she could see over the steering wheel *and* press the accelerator at the same time. Theresa wiped the tearstains from her cheeks with her T-shirt, put on a clean smile, and waved hello to her workmates, Justine and Dionne.

Justine attempted to fix her wind-blown hair while Dionne jumped out. "Hey, Theresa, coffee's on us! Look what I found." She waved a pound of Black Gold coffee beans from Della's Place in the air. In her best Juan Valdez accent, she pretended to read, "Fresh from the mountains of Colombia. Dark roast. Strong blend. Let no one sleep tonight!"

"That'll be a change," Theresa replied sarcastically. She had awakened at five o'clock this morning to a ringing telephone. "Oh, I'm sorry, were you asleep?" It was Foreign Affairs, oblivious to the time difference between Ontario and B.C.

"Check this out." Dionne poked the coffee package. "It says here on the label: Fair Trade Certified." She looked up at Theresa. "Only one hundred and ninety-nine more pounds of coffee in exchange for one Canadian diamond driller. Will's around two hundred, isn't he, Theresa? Sounds like a fair trade to me!"

Dionne led Theresa and Justine into the house — she knew her way to the coffee maker. They sat around the kitchen table as the coffee brewed. Then they soaked their conversation in the smell and taste and colour of Colombia.

Justine began. "Well, anything new?"

"Nope. I hope you didn't come over here for action."

Dionne piped up, "Hey, if we wanted action we'd go up the lake — I hear there's a party at the Armstrong cabin."

Theresa rolled her eyes. It helped to have friends who cared about her and knew what she was going through. She told them about being caught in the middle between Nick and Foreign Affairs. Because she feared for Will's safety, she had followed everyone's advice and done nothing. "Everyone tells me to be patient. But that's so hard. I seem to take it out on the kids."

"And the kids take it out on the dog. Isn't that right, Snorty?" Dionne rubbed the old dog's ears with her foot. Snorty lurked under the table, hopeful for a pat or a dropped morsel of food. He pushed back against her foot and wheezed contentedly.

"Isn't there anyone you can talk to who has been through this?" asked Justine. "Will can't be the first kidnapped man in Colombia."

"Unfortunately, he's the only one I know about. I contacted Adirondack Drilling — Will and Ted worked for them in Venezuela a few years ago. They said, 'Think of it like buying or selling a car. In the beginning, the guerrillas set an astronomical price. Then negotiations start.' They warned me not to expect anything soon — a minimum of three months. I just wish I knew he was alive."

All three looked into their coffee cups until Justine enquired about Michael.

Theresa laughed. "Michael said something funny to Belinda — remember Belinda with the Volkswagen van? Anyway, she brought over a little rear-view mirror for Michael's bike. He wondered what his dad would do when he ran out of underwear. So Belinda said, 'You know, Mike, your dad's a smart guy. It won't take him long to figure it out. He'll just turn them inside out.'"

The laughter felt good.

"And Kelly?"

"Kelly thinks about her dad every day. She helps around the house and walks Michael to swimming lessons. She takes a lot of calls for me... oh, that reminds me. Foreign Affairs called the other day. Kelly answered and explained, as she had the day before, that I was at work. They asked her for my work number, and Kelly said, 'I gave it to you two days ago.' And then she said, 'Write it down!'"

"Argh!" wailed Dionne. "We're becoming our mothers!"

"Where are the kids now?" asked Justine.

"Kelly's in a snit over at Kat's and Michael is playing over at Brennan's. Thank goodness for neighbours with kids. I'm not much fun these days." Justine and Dionne noticed Theresa's tears were never far away. Signs of strain lined her face.

"I hear the *Monarch Valley Press* wants to run a story," Justine said.

"Have you thought about it at all? A story from you might reroute some of the rumours going around."

Theresa chuckled. " Oh, you mean the one where Will's a big-time drug dealer and he finally got arrested in Colombia?"

"Yeah, that one got some mileage. Ah, small towns...." Dionne didn't have to finish the sentence.

Justine continued, "Well, it *is* the biggest story ever to hit Monarch Valley. And people are curious. If you put it in the paper, it might save you some time on the phone."

"I can't. If I spoke to one paper, then they'd *all* be after me. Some of these reporters are really rude and pushy. They don't seem to understand that I'm not a 'scoop.' I'm a person with feelings. I'm surprised the phone isn't ringing right now. "

"Do you think some local coverage might prompt Foreign Affairs? Sometimes a little pressure from the public can get some action. The current strategy doesn't seem to be getting Will any closer to home."

"They tell me things are happening out of the public eye. That's one thing Foreign Affairs, politicians, the police, and Nick all agree on: no press. They even tell me not to talk to anyone over the Internet. It could be monitored. Any comments could jeopardize Will's safety."

"Ah, the Internet. It's replaced the old Ford Fairlane — that's where we all learned about sex, right, Justine?"

Justine reddened. "Lord love a duck, Dionne."

"Oh, there's more than just sex on the Internet," Theresa said. "I've been getting stuff sent to me that says, 'You can hire mercenaries that will go wherever you want to rescue your loved one.'"

"Hey, that's good." Dionne said. "Don't forget to tell Jim Itch at Foreign Affairs that you hired one of these guys. That should get a rise out of the whole department."

— — —

Buzzing from the coffee, but happy to talk about Will with friends, Theresa washed out the mugs. Others could suggest going to the media; they had nothing to lose. She was afraid to do or say anything to anybody. On the other hand, maybe Foreign Affairs did need a prod. She felt like Sally Field in *Not Without My Daughter*. She had to make some life-or-death decisions, but how could she choose correctly when she had no control and didn't know who to trust? No. She had to remain patient and hopeful that people in Canada were at work with people in Colombia to have Will freed. At least until the next phone call.

Just like the unsprayed apples in the backyard, tunnels were being chewed through Theresa's insides. It was only a matter of time before something ugly surfaced.

FOURTEEN

"WHERE ARE YOU, YOU BASTARDS?"

The mountainside replied with indifferent silence. Nick examined his watch as the minute hand clawed its way to the top of the hour. Four o'clock. He plucked a dead butterfly by its long wings from the grill of the T-Rex four-by-four and slammed his fist down on the hood of the truck.

"It's another goddamn no-show. Fucked again." Nick's eyebrows knitted together to form a single dark slash across his forehead. He asked Alonso, "Can we make Bucaramanga by dark, or at least before the next bloody downpour?"

"If we take #22 and avoid the roadblock, we can make the Buca highway by dark," Alonso said. Casting an experienced eye on the clouds tumbling over the mountain behind them, he added, "No chance we'll miss the downpour."

"Christ almighty. We can't wait up here while the road washes out." He squashed his cigarette butt into the rocky soil.

Nick did not venture far without Alonso. The hard muscles covering Alonso's 6'4" frame belied a catlike agility, and Nick had never seen the man sleep. Nick depended on Alonso's loyalty, his local smarts, his concealed handgun, and the loaded sniper rifle in the truck. Two years in the Colombian army had taught Alonso how to take orders and keep his opinions to himself. Alonso allowed Nick to call it a day.

This particular day had started before sunrise, when Nick drove the T-Rex pick-up off the city's broken pavement into the mountains. He consulted a hand-drawn map on his cigarette package. Like many of the forestry roads in the mountains, the road they followed had been punched through after the topographical maps were made. Hastily built on the cheap, the road already showed signs of erosion. At the end of each switchback, Nick bounced the pick-up over a stream that should have run under a bridge or through a culvert. By mid-morning, they had reached the fork in the road described on the cigarette package, hardly visible through the thick, alder-like vegetation. Here they waited, expecting to meet with the guerrillas, until finally Nick had had enough. He would drive fearlessly over precipitous, crumbling, unmarked mountain roads, but to sit in one spot like a target made him nervous.

The bag of supplies Nick had packed for Will — painkillers, vitamins, extra clothes and work socks, a paperback novel — would remain undelivered. Nick jumped in behind the wheel and the truck roared to life. Alonso climbed aboard and rode shotgun, scanning the countryside while Nick vented.

"I checked that map a hundred times. The bastards know we're here! Why in hell don't they fuckin' show themselves?"

"The forest has eyes, sir."

"They're just testin' us. They wanna know we're clean. Tell me, does it look like we're concealin' a whole goddamn company of U.S. Marines?" Nick answered his own question with a "Fuck you miserable bastards!" aimed through his rolled-down window at the forest that refused to break its silence.

— — —

Like most businessmen, Nick detested red tape and unstable politics, and he liked to make money. For the Colombian division of T-Rex of Timmins, two out of three wasn't bad. During the last five years Nick adapted his company to fit Colombian protocol. He didn't care who ran right, who ran left, or what atrocities had been done to whom however long ago. He trusted his own instincts and a few good men because Colombia overflowed with opportunity for small drilling operations — smallness being key. A small company could be flexible, and flexibility meant survival when the rules (and the people who made them) changed so frequently.

Nick had grown up in Timmins. It was a good place to learn about the mining business, but it was about as exciting as a winter tire. He had also felt reined in there by responsibility, history, and cool relations with a hometown wife and family. To Nick, a guy who broke out in hives over multicoloured forms and hated scraping truck windows, Colombia felt like home. There was something intoxicating about steamy equatorial nights perfumed with jasmine, adventure, and sex — especially the nights he shared with his dance instructor, whose ample hips continued to sway long after the music ceased playing.

Unfortunately, this kidnapping thing threw Nick head-first into Colombia's political turmoil. Nick would not side with either party; his only allegiance was with his worker. If an employee was suffering because he had misjudged the situation, he knew the event could potentially ruin his business. But Nick also believed that a man's life and freedom superseded everything. After all, there were worse things than hitting rock bottom in the drilling business.

— — —

The rain had thinned to a drizzle by the time Nick and Alonso drove into the snarl of city traffic. They merged onto Calle San Michel, which took them to the centre of the city — the colonial-style *ciudad vieja*. The Hotel California was dark, and Sebastian's was closed for the night. No light shone from the second-floor window. It was too late to meet with the cigarette-pack artist, Agustín Pérez-Molero.

"Goddammit!" Nick threw his cigarette onto the wet pavement. Stars began to poke through the dark clouds above the quiet neon sign fixed to the side of the hotel. He and Alonso would have to get some answers from Agustín tomorrow. *Mañana.*

FIFTEEN

"IT'S NOT BAD ONCE YOU GET USED TO IT."

Where on the shores of Great Slave Lake had Will heard that before? Luis stood chest-deep in the near-freezing water, encouraging Will to join him. Even thirty-one days of stink, sweat, and blisters, plus two weeks of intestinal cramps and diarrhea, could not convince Will to take a cold bath.

José was already submerged. His thin brown arms pumped up and down, and his stringy hair flipped from side to side as he floundered through the water. Luis said to Will, "*Mira!* Free swimming lessons!"

Dry on his rock, Will ventured no further than his rolled-up pant-legs. He'd spent enough time in his life immersed in cold water to be immune to its appeal. Pensively, he looked through the reflection of a darkly bearded man to his soaking white feet.

The previous day, Will and the guerrilla group had tracked an energetic stream from swampy lowland to high alpine. Vines as thick as forearms tripped them as the guerrillas swung their machetes through vegetation so lush it was difficult to tell if the surrounding mist came from the sky or the earth. Five-foot-tall marijuana plants flourished amid the native vegetation. Large and small insects bit and sucked and chewed and crawled on any exposed flesh. Iguanas clamped to fat branches watched the commotion pass by with unblinking eyes.

It was nearly dark when they reached the source of the stream: a small, round glacier-fed lake surrounded by rocky peaks. Will was spent; he could barely hold his head high enough to take in the view. The breeze blowing off the lake carried the tantalizing smell of meat cooking. With renewed vigour, the troop followed the aroma to a two-storey stone house on the lakeshore. One by one, they passed through the thick doorway into the light and the wondrous smell.

A side of beef sizzled on a stone grill surrounded by roasted potatoes and platters of corn tortillas. Will looked at Luis, who looked at José in bewilderment. The soldiers, too, stood in awe until Anna, the woman in army fatigues supervising the feast, encouraged them to come and eat what they like: "*Tomen y coman, lo que quieran.*" She greeted El Capitán and the second-in-command with kisses on their cheeks. Again, the prisoners exchanged surprised glances.

The kitchen housed bags of rice, bins of corn, tubs of root vegetables, and jars of cornmeal, salt, flour, and sugar. Pots of herbs thrived on the wide windowsill. Skeins of chilis hung from the ceiling. Baskets overflowed with guavas, passion fruit, limes, and avocados. Will, Luis, José, and the soldiers filled their bowls and went outside to sit by the lake. Reflections of the crescent moon and a thousand southern stars jiggled on its surface. With his spoon and jackknife, Will cut into the succulent meat. He savoured the smell, tasted the flavour, and felt the texture as he rolled each bite of food around in his mouth before he swallowed. Simple things, like three clean utensils, Will had taken for granted a mere month ago. Knives, forks, and spoons. Home, love, and freedom. He missed them all so much.

The stone house appeared to be a rest stop for the guerrillas — a temporary place of peace. Throughout the week, Will saw troops arrive and others depart. They exchanged messages about friends and family. Inside the stone house, soldiers became ordinary people who told stories to each other and laughed out loud. Will suspected that some of these young people became soldiers not out of a desire to fight, but a yearning for companionship. The guerrilla movement was its own community.

One night, a crowd of soldier boys gathered around a transistor radio. Amid the static, or maybe it was cheering, Will could hear the sound of a baseball game. The commentator's voice sent Will back to the year that he and Michael, only three at the time, had bet on the Toronto Blue Jays to win the World Series. Everyone else bet on the Phillies. The series came down to one pitch. When Joe Carter hit his game-winning home run, Will and Michael also won. The pot was big enough for a new car-shaped bed with wheels and a race-car quilt.

Despair began to grow as he thought about his kids growing up without him. Will left the baseball game, certain that childhood was too short for jungle war games, no matter whose side you were on.

Every day, Will was reminded that he was a prisoner deprived of the things in life that had value. He and Luis had become good friends — together they had washed in streams, squatted in bushes, built calluses, took orders, lost weight, and grown beards. Luis had a practicality that Will appreciated, and he never tired of listening to Will's stories about the untamed mining world, filled with money, liquor, women, and jail cells. But their friendship was also the only thing of value they now possessed, and Will feared that someday his captors could use it against them.

Will was also reminded of his imprisonment when El Capitán and the second-in-command climbed upstairs to what he assumed was the radio room. To these men, he represented foreign control and all the evils of the capitalist system. He was merely a tool to be used to bring money to the organization. Throughout his working life, Will had considered work and politics a bad combination: Now here he was, proof of his own belief, in that his value as a man had been reduced to the colour of a poker chip.

— — —

Seven days at the stone house cured Will of his fleas and allowed some of his insect bites to scab over. Unfortunately, being stationary in this warped, homelike setting also gave him time to think about the freedoms that had been taken away from him. He lagged behind the others, who walked down the mountain as if a destination lay before them, seemingly rejuvenated by the combination of fresh fish and dry underwear. His time at the stone house reminded Will that the longer he remained a captive, the less likely it seemed that someone would put up the money for him. He didn't want that someone to be Theresa. Most of their money was tied up in their house, and Will did not want her to mortgage it over him. She had worked too hard for that to happen. He searched for the strength to control his despair, but that was becoming ever more difficult as the days dragged on. Again, he turned his concentration toward the trail in front of him.

The footpath told Will that life in rural Colombia depended upon the land. People walked in this country, just as he had walked in rubber boots through sucking muskeg, in winter boots over snow that squawked, in bare feet over dandelions and dirt roads. Will and his brother and sisters not only played outside, but slept, ran, lit fires, rode broken bikes, made rafts, flipped canoes, and nearly died several times outside as well. Even in the winter, they played and worked outside. He remembered how the sweat would run down his arms into his hands as he chopped wood under brilliant winter constellations in the minus-forty air.

Will recalled moose-hunting with his father during the winter's first snowfall. Overnight, the yellow, warm, earthy world turned silent, cold, and blue. No longer could the moose hide from its own tracks. His mother taught him how to cure the hide, which she later fashioned for the boys into fringed, knee-high moccasins. She taught them which plants to brew for tea, how to identify edible mushrooms, where to look for blueberries, and once, how to remove a fish hook from his little brother's foot. He had always hoped to pass on his love of the outdoors to Michael and Kelly, a task that now seemed impossible in his absence.

Communication between soldiers and prisoners was nonexistent when El Capitán was around. When the commander wasn't in sight, Will found he could talk to Francisco. The other soldier boys had difficulty understanding his Spanish and didn't even try. The only time they spoke to him was to joke about Monica Lewinsky and her affair with President Clinton. It didn't matter how many times Will explained the difference between the U.S. and Canada; their knowledge of the world would not extend beyond their surroundings.

Will asked Francisco, who wore his Che bandana tied around his arm today, "What if the army catches the farmers growing these crops?" Will referred to the fields of slender bushes with small bright green leaves concealed by scraggly rows of corn.

"Oh, *es muy malo*," Francisco replied. "*Señor Eduardo*, one good field of coca can buy many things for many years." He told Will that such crops grew twice as fast as other crops, didn't require special tools, and incurred no overhead costs. Will asked about the paperwork.

"What do you mean, paperwork?" Francisco asked.

Will shook his head, and Francisco went on to explain to Will, who already knew, that growing coca made money. Farmers got paid in cash. "But," he continued, "sometimes the paramilitary spy on our fields. Then they burn them or spray them with orange chemical, and then nothing grows." Francisco blamed the War on Drugs, claiming that the Colombian government received millions of dollars from the United States and encouraged these so-called "cleansing rounds." Francisco puzzled over the connection. "We are a poor country. You are so rich and have everything you want. Why do you need to take the drugs?"

Will couldn't answer. He suspected the guerrillas pressured the farmers to grow illegal crops as well, throwing the *campesinos* into the middle of the armed conflict. Too much money was at stake, no matter how socialistic the cause. He didn't say anything to Francisco when they passed a group of warehouses crammed with bricks of marijuana shrink-wrapped in plastic and ready for transport. Farming was a dangerous occupation in Colombia — no wonder so many of the farmhouses they passed appeared empty.

— — —

At a branch in the trail, Jesús turned off with a spring in his step. Francisco pointed to a small house almost invisible against the treed background. A trail of smoke could be traced to a black mound of charcoal in the yard. "Jesús lives there."

The small farm gave the illusion that rural life had not changed for a hundred years. One mango tree shaded the entire cinderblock house. A rusty, corrugated metal roof extended over a porch crowded with hammocks, chairs, and a table. Chickens pecked the ground around the yard, and a milk cow grazed in tall grass. The fields around the house were as large as what a family with hand tools could manage. Will supposed the cart beside the water tank was more reliable than access to gasoline.

Jesús melted into a cluster of brown people. Children grabbed at his hands until he lifted a tiny person onto his shoulders. An older man in a straw hat walked toward him with a scythe over his shoulder. Will stared at the scene and swallowed. He was overwhelmed with despair. It sucked the air from the bottom of his lungs and he wondered if he could even walk.

— — —

Later that day, Francisco and Alejandro sat in with the captives for games of gin rummy during their break. "*Cuarenta y ocho y otro catorce es, mmm...es, mmm...*" Francisco tried to add forty-eight and fourteen together on his fingers. "*Setenta y dos. Es correcto, Señor Eduardo?*"

Will corrected him, "*No, es sesenta y dos.*" *Sixty-two, not seventy-two.* Will shot a look over to Luis that said, "I think he knows more than he pretends." He gathered the cards, shuffled, and dealt five hands.

From out of nowhere, the second-in-command broke into their card game. Francisco and Alejandro picked up their rifles and left in haste. The three prisoners looked up at the authoritative figure who waved a school notebook at them. With his stubby index finger, the second-in-command tore out three pages and handed one to each of them. The outside world needed to know they were alive. He outlined the rules: "*Escriban una carta. No comunicación en clave.*" *Write a letter. No secret codes. No revealing location.* They were also to write down where they were born as a kind of identification key.

"This is a good sign, *amigo*," Luis whispered to Will. "Someone negotiates for us. They want proof of life so that people on the outside will pay whatever they ask." Luis put his pencil to paper and wrote his message to Heidi, Uli, and Damien.

Will chewed his pencil. The empty, wide-lined page stared up at him. Did he dare believe Luis? He doubted that this letter would end up in Theresa's hands. But just in case it did, he began: "Dear Theresa, Kelly, and Michael."

He worked on the next line: "How are you? How's old Snorty? I am fine." Then he was stuck. If he wrote too much, the guards would think he was relaying information. How do you tell the people you love that you love them? He decided upon the direct approach. "I love you and I miss you all. Try not to worry about me. Love, Will (Dad)."

Maybe Zhuri's mule would carry his letter down the mountain. It would flit and dart like a butterfly past the army checkpoints. Then it would fly a slow and straight flight pattern to Canada. Maybe Jenna MacIntosh, the girl with the smiling eyes at the Monarch Valley Post Office, would place it in his family's post box. Maybe Theresa would pick it up and bring it home. Home.

Will's eyes narrowed. He snapped his pencil in half with the fingers of one hand as he returned his page to the second-in-command. Should his letter reach Theresa and the kids, he bloody well wanted to be there to read it to them.

SIXTEEN

SHE NEEDED OUT. And the kids really needed out. At least that's what Belinda told Theresa while she drove her Volkswagen van, nicknamed "Pookie," along the twisted lake road to the beach. It was a sweltering August day. Unfortunately for the five sweaty occupants, Pookie predated air conditioning, so when Belinda's van wheezed into the parking lot, everyone rejoiced.

Belinda's sixteen-year-old son Grease launched himself explosively from the sliding door of the flowered van, with Michael right behind him. Kelly protested that Michael wasn't carrying his fair share as she, Theresa, and Belinda loaded up with umbrellas, towels, coolers, and beach bags.

Their flip-flops snapped along the marijuana-scented boardwalk down to the public beach, where giant Ponderosa pines framed an image Norman Rockwell might have painted: People of all sizes and ages mixed together like a summer salad, enjoying the cool water and the warm, sandy beach.

Sphinxlike granite boulders jutted into the water from both points of the sandy crescent. Theresa could see Michael, in the midst of his buddies, clambering his way up the rocks on all fours. Kelly stopped to join a well-oiled group of teenagers playing volleyball. Grease was nowhere to be seen; Belinda doubted that he got past the boardwalk. The two friends dumped their gear, spread towels on the sand, and propped up the sun umbrella. Belinda reached into her bag for sunscreen.

"Do you need any of this goop while I have it out, Theresa?"

"No thanks. I'm covered." Despite her dark eyes and dark hair, Theresa burned easily. She had always envied Will and Michael's ability to turn brown in the sunshine. With closed eyes she released a long sigh and wallowed in the warmth of the sand beneath her towel as it moulded to the shape of her body. "You were right, Be. We needed this. It's the first time all three of us have been away from the phone together for an entire afternoon."

"I know, it's about time you agreed to come out. It's summertime, and at this latitude, summer is short enough. The kids need to have some fun with you."

"This will be the time I get the phone call."

"You know what you need?" Belinda said. "A shoe-phone. Remember? From *Get Smart?*"

Theresa smiled. "Yes, I remember. A great idea, except what happens when you want to wear sandals?"

"Yeah, that's a problem. Someone needs to invent a mobile phone small enough to fit into a purse."

Theresa thought of her teenage daughter. "Could be a big market out there for it."

Both women closed their eyes and let the sun massage warmth into their bodies.

"It's been a while since we've had coffee. How are you holding up, Theresa?"

"You know, I'm doing better."

"Really?"

"Well, I'm seeing somebody." Belinda's jaw dropped. "Oh, jeez — that's not what I mean. I mean I'm *seeing* somebody...."

"Yeah, I got that part."

"Somebody I never would have expected. He's a healer. Well, he's not really a healer, but he sees things. He knew that I hadn't heard anything from or about Will."

"Yeah?"

"He wanted me to bring him something of Will's. So I did."

"You didn't give him any money, did you?"

"No, no, no. We met at the used bookstore — you know, the one with the comfy chairs across from the pottery studio? I brought Will's spare pair of glasses from the glove compartment and his glasses case."

"So what happened?"

"He held Will's glasses in his hands."

"Uh-huh."

"He said they were warm."

"What did he mean by that?"

Theresa looked directly at Belinda. "It means Will's still alive."

"That's incredible." Belinda paused. She spoke slowly, choosing her words carefully. "Couldn't the glasses be warm from being in the car?"

"No," Theresa answered. "It was cool that day. I know you're skeptical, but I believe him."

"Who is this mystic man?"

"I can't tell you, but you know him very well. He has this gift — but no one would ever suspect it. The feelings are so intense I think they frighten him."

"That's too bizarre."

"Belinda, this whole thing is bizarre, starting with my dream the day Will was kidnapped." Theresa turned cold with the memory. "Kelly's behaviour at the airport was weird — she's never clung to Will like that before. Then Will's sister believed that good news was coming to Monarch Valley... everything tells me that Will's okay. That's why I'm better. Call it superstition, call it what you want, but I just don't have anything more concrete than that to go on." Theresa sat up and dug a magazine out of her beach bag. "I'm even going to church on Sundays. Our pastor drops by every now and then to say hi and ask how I'm doing."

"Pastor Higgins?"

"Yes. He's always good to talk to. The only problem is he comes when I'm out in the garden, and I'm wearing something like this...." Belinda laughed with Theresa as parts of her rounded figure spilled out of her bathing suit. "So I'm always a bit sidetracked trying to find a shirt to put on while he talks. But he cares about us, and I can always count on him if things get bad."

They watched the activity on the lake. Michael and his friends had found a raft full of girls that needed tipping.

"Faith and faith healers — I guess they both provide crutches when you haven't got much to stand on," Belinda mused. "So what's with those guys down south? Can't they give you any news about Will?"

"Nope. No word." Theresa sighed. "This has been the longest five weeks of my life. Ted calls every other night — bless his heart. He told me Nick went up into the mountains to talk with the guerrillas. But they never showed up."

"I don't get it. How did these guerrilla groups get to be so power- ful? What do they want with Will?"

"It's not Will they want. It's money. And forget good intentions. It's called greed. People get kidnapped all the time, and not just by the guerrillas. I've cashed in my term deposits and moved what investments we had into a money market so when the call comes, I'll be ready. Will's sisters contributed to the fund at the reunion and I've decided to mortgage the house."

"Whoa — Theresa, I didn't know that...." They watched a couple of Jet Skis race across the bay. "Those annoying machines are spreading like smallpox." In the same tone, Belinda continued, "And where the hell is Foreign Affairs these days?"

"Good question. I honestly don't expect anything from them since they told me, 'We don't talk to terrorists.' How will anything change if people don't talk to one another?"

Belinda agreed. "Maybe we need more women in charge."

"Just someone who could talk *and* listen would help. At least I talk to the same department person now, so I don't have to repeat myself as often. And Jim Itch — Dionne stuck him with that name — finally stopped asking me why I let Will go to Colombia when I told him, 'That's the type of work he does. My husband is a driller.' You know, in the beginning, I figured they would know what to do. I thought they could investigate wrongfully kidnapped, or accused, or jailed Canadians. Every phone call, I swear I give them more information about Colombia than they give me. I got so upset the last time Foreign Affairs phoned, I cleaned my oven."

"Eww — I've never been that upset. Sounds like they're trying to politically correct themselves into a state of uselessness until the situation resolves itself. I wonder who's running our Foreign Affairs these days."

"I think they're more concerned about covering their butts than getting Will out of Colombia. You know, I'm not the first person this has happened to. Some days I just don't want to wake up. I worry about the kids. But the worst part is, I feel so alone. If anyone else out there has gone through all this, I'd really like to talk to them. Maybe they want to talk to me. I even asked Jim Itch, 'Isn't there anyone else in Canada that this has happened to?'"

"What'd he say?"

"He wouldn't tell me. He just gave me the same old song and dance about what Foreign Affairs can and cannot do. He wants me to think he's doing me a favour. Then he tells me not to go to the media. He said, 'If the media gets going on this, they'll turn it into a three-ring circus.'"

"So what are you supposed to do when the phone rings and it's the *Globe and Mail*, or *Rolling Stone*?"

"He says I'm supposed to give the reporter the number for Foreign Affairs."

Belinda started laughing. "Really? I can hardly wait for the photographs. Jim Itch in his ringmaster costume."

Theresa laughed too. "I picture him more as Lily Tomlin at the switchboard, plugging in *People* and unplugging the *New York Times*."

"Line busy... line busy?" Belinda snorted.

The women were now drawing looks from the people around them, their tears of laughter dropping into the hot sand. A stampede of sun-soaked volleyball players charged past them for the water.

"Check out those tight little bums, will ya?" Belinda remarked.

"Yeah, wouldn't it be great to go back in time to when your hair mattered? How did we sleep in those soup-can rollers?"

"I didn't use rollers — I ironed mine. Hey, I'm fine with forty. See these white hairs? It's the new blonde. Go ahead, sun and gravity — I give you my body!" Belinda turned to Theresa and lifted up her sunglasses. "Oh, if I wrinkle up and get blown away, help yourself to some cherries from my tree before The Stomach That Walks raids the cooler."

Theresa did, careful not to bite any cherries in half. She admired the mountain view across the lake. For the first time, she noticed the smooth ridges above the tree line that joined mountain to mountain. Mountain to mountain, mountain to mountain, as far to the south as the eye could see.

SEVENTEEN

IT WAS A SLOW GAME IN THE STILL AIR. Will and Luis played cards during an afternoon break because cards did not require energy. José dozed against his pack. They had been moving daily from camp to camp since their week of respite at the stone house.

Luis sighed, and hung his head. "I am weary of all of this, Will. It's been thirty-eight days and we are still here." The cards stuck to each other.

"Things take time, Luis." Will leaned back on his pack. "Your organization has to notice you and José are missing. It takes time to figure out where you are. It takes more time to establish contact with these guys, even with their big radios. Don't worry, Luis. Someone's cutting a deal for you as I try to shuffle this deck of cards."

Luis looked away. "Do you know what I want when we get out, Will?"

"Freedom to take a piss alone?"

"I'm a socialist, Will. I believe a good society is like a community dinner where everyone contributes and everyone benefits. It has the presence of justice, and the absence of fear. I can remember Allende's last live broadcast before the CIA shot him on September 11, 1973. Immediately following his speech, the tanks rolled into Santiago and a democratically elected government was replaced with a military regime as easily as you change the sheets on a bed. People who dared to speak out were 'disappeared.' So many people disappeared that the verb became a noun, *los desaparecidos*."

Will listened, but he was tired. He looked up and wondered how clouds so bottom-heavy stayed afloat. He longed for a breath of crisp September morning air. When the conversation turned political, Luis could ramble on for hours.

"I suspect my parents had some foresight — that is why they sent me to Germany." Luis looked into the distance and went on. "Heidi and I listened to the BBC World Service after midnight, but the news from home lacked any substance. Journalists either became accessories of the military or escaped to the Brazilian jungle. Because the media did not reflect the truth, we became proficient at speaking in cartoons, poems, and songs. My parents denied the reports about brutality and torture. To this day, I have no idea how involved my father was — I'm sure my mother doesn't know either. We heard the Secret Service drove around in Ford Falcons and knocked on doors late at night. I remember Father's private secretary owned one of those cars. It was green."

Will removed his hat and fanned himself with it.

"Without a voice, there is no justice. Without justice, there is no peace." Luis looked at his cards despairingly. "And Pinochet, the greatest silencer of all time, remains a free man."

"I'm not sure if you'll find the place you're looking for, Luis," said Will, touching an old scar on his cheek. He tried diverting Luis' attention back to the card game. "Three of a kind! You are one lucky son of a bitch today." Will stared at his own bleak hand. A fat drop of sweat splashed onto a black deuce.

Francisco appeared before the card players. "*Señor José, Señor Luis, Señor Eduardo*. Time to go."

Luis pocketed the cards. With great effort they hoisted their packs onto their backs, still dark with sweat, and resumed their positions in line. A hard rain began to fall.

"No luck today, *Señor Eduardo*?" asked Francisco.

"Oh, there was lots of luck today, Frank. None of it mine." He hated to lose. Why had the cards turned on him?

— — —

They hadn't walked far when José stopped. Because of his position at the front, everyone else stopped too. They moved their heads around each other to see José kneel down and dig his fingers into the muddy ground. He uncovered a small horseshoe and held it up. The rain washed over it. Through his mud-splattered glasses, Will witnessed a miracle. The dull, pathetic thing turned into a silver holy relic. José crossed himself and kissed the horseshoe while he murmured, "*Gracias, Virgen de Guadalupe, gracias!*"

Two minutes down the trail, Luis uncovered his own horseshoe. He called ahead to Will: "You were right, I am a lucky *hijo de puta* today!" With both of his hands, he presented his prize to the black-ened sky. Will saw profound gratitude on Luis' wet, tear-stained face.

Will chastised himself. How could he have missed the second horseshoe? He must have walked right over it, unable to see through the streaks on his glasses. The right side of his brain — he called it the white side — told him superstitions and lucky charms did not exist. But the native side of his brain believed. He focused his eyes on the ground before his feet, willing them to recover a third silver horseshoe.

That evening, huddled under the camp kitchen tarp, Will ate

a damp and tasteless meal of noodles, black beans, and slivers of corned beef. He listened to Luis and José prattle on about their discoveries. "The horseshoes are omens that tell us we will soon be free — I can feel it right here." José said, thumping his soggy chest.

"You Latinos are *locos*," Will said. "I think you're setting yourselves up for one hell of a crash."

"*No, amigo. No estamos locos.* I feel it too." Luis sounded absurdly serious to Will.

"Funny thing. I felt the same thing a month ago. Remember that pork that hung too long? I had the shits for a week."

"Tomorrow will be your lucky day, my friend." Luis patted Will's back. "We will help you find your own horseshoe."

"Good. And maybe we'll have rum and Coca-Cola after we dance the *merengue*." Will lumbered off to wash his dishes and brush his teeth in the creek. He could hear José and Luis chumming with El Capitán and the second-in-command long into the drippy evening.

When Luis and José joined Will in their tent, Will was irate. Only sleep could relieve the pain in his hips, and he could not sleep. The two South Americans tossed restlessly.

"What the hell is with you guys?" Will asked.

Luis finally answered him. "El Capitán said the German government has connected our release with foreign aid to Colombia."

"What does that have to do with the guerrillas?"

"Everything, my good friend. Everything," Luis replied.

Will stared long into the darkness while the forest dripped down the canvas sides of their tent. Luis and José belonged to a team of people who brought expertise and outside attention to river restoration — specifically the Rio de Oro. Money from the German government paid for extensive river and stream clean-up, which the guerrillas, who were also the locals, appreciated. Will had overheard the leaders talk about the merits of the river projects — he knew they wouldn't want projects with a humanitarian focus to be dismantled. Someone within their organization had established contact and come to an agreement with the guerrillas. If Luis and José were freed, allowed to go home, to walk away, Will thought, what would happen to him?

— — —

The next morning, Will woke to a cacophony of sounds he had heard many times before in tropical locations. He moved the tent flap aside and looked into the tall shade trees occupied by a group of agitated howler monkeys. The monkeys rained broken branches down upon the tents, thumped their chests, whooped and hooted, and peed on them from their high perches. At ground level, Francisco, Alejandro, Jesús, Juan, and Miguel mirrored the primates. They jumped around, dragged their knuckles on the ground, laughed, thumped, and hooted, which further aggravated the family of monkeys. Will too.

Stiff and sore from a poor sleep, Will dragged himself out of his tent and sat expressionless while the pandemonium raged around him. He was tired of the company of children with guns in the jungle.

After his breakfast of boiled rice, Will rolled up the groundsheet for the thirty-ninth time, cheered on by the howler monkeys. Fully loaded, soldiers and prisoners waited for the command that did not come. El Capitán and the second-in-command were conspicuously absent.

Will sat in the shade against his pack and watched Francisco clean his rifle. His slender brown hands encouraged the steel grey parts to glide together. Each piece clicked into place with authority. The boy was trying to whistle. Will imagined the graceful hands inserting batteries into a remote-controlled airplane destined to buzz around a schoolyard. Will sighed. He had played enough cowboys and Indians in his youth to know when it was time to call the game and go home.

"You're lazy, Frank. It's your job to tell us to move. What's going on this morning?"

"I don't know, *Señor Eduardo*. I wait for my orders."

The other soldiers smoked, spoke quietly to one another, watched the sky. Their lifestyle had trained them how to wait. The army didn't have to. When El Capitán and the second-in-command reappeared with the radio, the cool part of the day was gone. Will stood up, anxious to leave and move onto the next camp.

Two big blue butterflies fluttered through the clearing. Will swatted at them with the back of his hand. The butterflies, caught up in the business of mating, did not notice the indelicate attempt on their lives. They twirled and bumped together soundlessly in their careless dance across the clearing to the tall trees.

When the order to move finally came, Will walked between Francisco and Alejandro, his eyes on the ground, in search of the silver talisman that would promise him freedom.

— — —

After the evening rice and beans, El Capitán and the second-in-command invited Luis and José to their radio conference. Will could hear them talking, but they were too far away for him to hear the details. He assumed their price had been met. Alone in front of his tent, Will was unable to write the day's entry in his diary before he went to bed.

Later that night, Luis and José came into the tent and lay down. Luis spoke to Will. "They are going to split us up. José and I are slated to join another group. We'll be leaving at five in the morning."

A large moon shone through the trees and the tent wall. José and Luis lay on the groundsheet, smoking the cigarettes they had earned for good behaviour. They lit new cigarettes with the ends of old ones. Will watched the moon slide across his side of the tent as he feigned sleep. He knew there was no other group — Luis must have been told to say that. He was too close to freedom to disobey an order.

Several cigarettes later, they heard a short whistle. Luis and José pushed their belongings out of the tent and crawled into a wash of moonlight. Will could see four pairs of boots through the space between the tent canopy and the ground. Army-issue towels, blankets, and toothbrushes fell on the ground. El Capitán's raspy voice was barely audible above the sounds of the night insects. Luis' German-made boots stood closest to the tent. Will fired his arm out from under the canopy, and grabbed Luis' ankle above his boot. He whispered hoarsely, "I know you are going home. When you get to Bucaramanga, call my brother Ted. Tell him not to worry about me. He's at the Hotel California."

The butt end of a rifle came down on his wrist, and Will pulled his arm back. The army boots rapidly stepped away from the tent. The German-made boots paused briefly.

A whisper: "I will find your brother Ted. Goodbye, *amigo*."

Luis' words were as soft as a butterfly landing on an outstretched hand. But unlike the lingering smoke trapped by the tent cover, the words escaped. They floated up and up and up, above the leafy canopy until they dissolved into the silver air.

EIGHTEEN

AGUSTÍN DREW THE FOLDING WALL across the front of the restaurant and hung up the CERRADO sign. Overhead, the buzz from the
neon fizzled and died. Sebastian's was closed to the public in order to
host a private function that demanded maximum security. Agustín
would consider yesterday's threatening phone call later. Today, he had
five special meals to prepare, and no time to answer messages from
DAS, the civilian intelligence service. Inside the restaurant, Nick,
Alonso, Uncle Oscar, and Ted, sat at a table with a well-groomed
gentleman named Luis.

Agustín had sent out an SOS to Mercedes so that he could relieve
his kitchen staff for the day. The less Noella and Elizabeth knew
about politically tainted events associated with Sebastian's, the safer
they all would be. Mercedes had arrived a few hours early to help
with preparation.

"So how long was this Luis held captive?" she whispered to Agustín when he entered the kitchen.

He pulled on his elbow-length oven mitts and prodded the fire in the *parrilla* with the long-handled poker. A bed of charcoal glowed red and orange in the firebox under the grill. "Forty days. The cell that released him is the same cell that has Will Edwards, the Canadian driller."

"I see. And is that the driller's brother?" Her eyes moved over the high counter that separated kitchen from the dining area. "The stocky fellow with the dark hair and big grin?"

"Yes. That's Ted Edwards." Agustín squeezed another lime into the fish marinade. "The man smoking, with his back against the wall, is Nick. He owns the drilling company Will and Ted worked for."

"He doesn't look like a wealthy man. And why doesn't he take off that filthy hat?"

"He's no tycoon, and he flunked Etiquette 101. His business is small. He manages two or three drilling crews, owns a minimal amount of equipment, some trucks, some camp gear. His office is in the Santa Clara district — a long way from downtown. He's the guy who put up bail for Alonso and me a couple of years ago. No questions asked. I respect the man — I'd call him a well-principled maverick. Just don't tell him he can't do something or, God forbid, direct him onto what he thinks is the wrong road. That's Alonso beside him. You remember him?"

"Yes. I don't remember him being so well-built, though."

"He's in the personal protection business now — works for Nick. He put his two years into the army after high school and then became a bodyguard. I used to kid him about his *mossels*." Agustín flexed his biceps for Mercedes and winked as he reached into the freezer for five tall glasses. "Thanks again for coming here on short notice. I love you."

"You'd better. I'm not cheap." She snapped on a pair of rubber gloves for emphasis and began to wash the lettuce.

Agustín removed his apron and pulled down his sleeves. "Kitchen is yours, baby. I'm goin' out — cover me." As if his tray, loaded with two imported beers, three Aguilas, and five glasses, were an extension of his arm, Agustín kissed his girlfriend and waltzed into the dining area. She smiled over the high counter and turned on the warming lights.

Agustín's fingerprints pressed through the dew of each tall glass as he poured the beer. The five celebrants clinked their glasses together and cheered. "A libertad!"

"Ahh," Luis said, his upper lip moist. "That is good. Thank you, gentlemen. I am honoured to share your company at the Hotel California. It is a relief to do as I please, go where I please, and eat lunch with whomever I please." Luis lifted his glass again. Ted drained his, thrilled to be with a man who had spoken to his brother fewer than forty-eight hours ago.

Luis looked directly at Ted. "You should know Will is in good health. As far as prisoners go, we were treated well. The guerrillas never threatened us with beatings or torture, and we were never tied up or chained. We all received the same portions of food — including the leaders. If Will needs medical attention—bandages, pills, antibiotics — he will get it. One of the guerrilla soldiers was a nurse and gave us all yellow fever shots." Relief washed over Ted's face.

Agustín described the specials he had prepared, gave the men time to choose, then retreated to the kitchen. Nick stubbed out his cigarette.

Luis apologized for his lack of knowledge about his release. "Will's last words to us were, 'Tell my brother Ted not to worry.' I know he wants you to pass that on to Theresa, Kelly, and Michael." Ted grinned; Oscar shared his happiness.

Luis was impeccably dressed, having spent the previous day buying clothes for his new lean shape. He enjoyed his first bath nearly as much as his first shave with a sharp blade. From an extensive bald patch, wisps of hair had been tied into a thin tail that fell past his collar. "It'll take Heidi back to 1973," he said. His brown eyes shone.

While delicious cooking smells wafted into the dining area, Luis spoke candidly about his days in captivity. "For us, boredom was a greater challenge than fear," he said, looking beyond the white curtains. "When a man is captured, he has only his imagination and his memories. These two things keep us human, and they keep us hoping." He then turned to Oscar for an update on the world of *fútbol*.

Agustín arrived with his arms full. He set down the entrées and removed the stainless steel covers reflecting the smiling faces gathered around the table. Ted had chosen the Argentine beefsteak; Luis, Nick, Alonso, and Uncle Oscar the *pescado del día*. His eyes closed, Luis breathed in the full aroma of the grilled fish. He said it was the scent of lime that made his eyes water. Agustín refilled the water glasses as Luis said, "Will was a good friend. He was correct in that you don't have to worry about him. He is a good hostage."

"A good hostage?" Ted asked.

"The soldiers all admired his ability to keep up without complaint despite his age. They called him *hombre viejo*, or old man, a term of respect in our country. The leaders cannot dislike him. He follows orders and he will not attempt anything that might get him killed. His greatest battle will be to stay hopeful about his release.

"We don't appreciate freedom until we lose it. And when we do, it requires colossal effort to keep hopelessness at bay. I am extremely thankful we had each other. Will talked freely with the guerrillas — more than José or I ever did. This was something I learned from your brother, Ted. I am convinced that if we talk to each other, at every level, there is hope for the peace process."

Luis managed to complete his meal between questions. When he finished, he wiped his mouth with the white linen napkin. Nick balled his up and put it on his empty plate, which was pushed aside to make room for the clean ashtray. Agustín then returned to the kitchen with a stack of dishes that was sure to make Mercedes grimace. When he came back with the dessert choices, the table was covered by a topographical map. As Alonso slowly ran the palm of his hand down the centre crease, Nick impatiently asked, "Does anything look familiar?"

Luis circled an area with his index finger and tapped the map with a clean fingernail. "Here's the Rio de Oro, the Arauca, and the Venezuelan border. The jeep carried us up here, well, partway up here. We walked for a day this way, and then back this way."

Agustín could see Nick using the map's contour lines to visualize the scenery from ground level. Nick looked at Agustín as if to say, "You didn't fuck up, you lucky son of a bitch." This settled the dispute over the cigarette pack drawing.

"Isn't this Frederico Constanza's territory?" Nick looked at Alonso, then to Agustín, and then to Luis. Without showing any sign of recognition, Agustín looked at the map. He held his breath, waiting for Luis to respond.

"Frederico Constanza?" Luis tried to recall some mention of the name. "Maybe. Will called him "El Capitán" and no one ever corrected him. I don't know the name of the second-in-command either, but the end of his index finger is missing. The nights we could hear baseball games on the soldiers' radios, Will joked about the short-fingered fastball. Will's sense of humour and his ability, as you say in English, to 'go with the flow' will help him bear any hardship."

"Frederico Constanza and Simón Bolívar Juárez," Alonso said. He knew those names, and so did Agustín, though he was careful to conceal his inside knowledge about the ARA from Uncle Oscar. "The cells move around so that no one knows exactly where they are, or who they are," he explained.

Nick's dark eyebrows untangled themselves. "Now we know who we're dealin' with. Thank Christ. Far as I know, Constanza's group doesn't deal drugs big-time." Alonso folded the map and tucked it into his briefcase.

Agustín counted three *pastels de tres leches* for dessert and left to prepare after-dinner *tintos y cafés*.

Luis touched Ted's arm. "I have a Lufthansa ticket to Frankfurt," he said. "I really can't stay. But there is one more thing Will taught us: a new card game."

"Gin rummy?"

"Yes!" Luis laughed. "I feel like I know you. Will told some remarkable stories about you both that kept our spirits alive. Your brother is a good man, and he is smart enough not to do the wrong thing." Ted nodded in agreement. He knew his brother was smart.

Luis apologized for parting company so quickly, but everyone understood.

Nick's eyebrows fused together again as he spoke to Ted and Oscar. "We're workin' on the financials right now. Alonso and I are headed for Venezuela next week. Maybe we'll swing by Aruba. I hear our good friend Mr. Blackburn likes to gamble in fancy places." Nick stubbed out his cigarette with finality.

Agustín returned to the kitchen, the empty coffee cups clattering against the dessert plates. Mercedes sweated over the sink, suds up to her elbows. Agustín kissed her again. "You should never have dropped out of restaurant management, my lovely." She shot him a dour look and said this was precisely why she dropped out. Agustín unbuttoned his cuffs and rolled up his long white sleeves.

Before Luis left Sebastian's, Agustín followed him into the *servicios para caballeros*. They were alone in the men's room.

"We are all relieved and thankful that you are back safely," Agustín said. *"Gracias* for bringing us news of Will Edwards."

"De nada. It is a pleasure to be able to eat at a fine restaurant such as this. I hope the business works out well for you."

"I have one question for you about Constanza's group."

"Certainly."

"How is my sister?"

NINETEEN

THE GUERRILLAS MARCHED for twenty-two hours to distance themselves as swiftly as possible from the hostage release location. It was
after three the next morning when they stopped. Will dropped to
the ground and slept. He couldn't recall any soldier girl removing
his yellow muckers. The long hike had been mercifully numbing.

The second day alone, Will slept. The soldiers put up his tent
around him.

The third day alone, he left his tent for the midday meal. He'd
never had armadillo before; it tasted rubbery. As he chewed, he could
see Francisco, Alejandro, and Carolina standing in the shade picking
dark red coffee berries. Will looked around and realized the camp
had been set up in a coffee plantation. Several giant trees spread
their limbs over the entire field, shading an unkempt plantation of

coffee bushes. Each bush was about two metres tall and covered with fruit. It was an ideal hiding place. Will watched the soldiers fill the bellies of their shirts and then dump their caches into burlap sacks. He thought about downtown Vancouver's trendy coffee shops and wondered if they charged extra for "guerrilla harvested."

Beyond the plantation, Will identified a scattering of orange and banana trees. A farmhouse with a collapsed roof leaned against a skeletonized tree. The house was made of wood, with a mud and stone foundation, and looked as if it was being broken apart and held together at the same time by a wild tangle of green.

Will sat in front of his tent for the rest of the afternoon, cross-legged, hands folded. He watched Jesús and Miguel dig the latrine pit — a sure sign of temporary permanence. Already they had occupied Camp Coffee for three days.

The fourth day alone, Will sat in front of his tent in the same way. He listened to the birds calling to one another. One song led to a scarlet bird, brazen against the green foliage of the creek that was also the source of their water. Just above the stream, metallic blue butterflies, as large as his hand, fluttered in the sunshine and disappeared into the shadows. Magical, carefree, and taunting.

Will considered his situation again. Only Blackburn could pay the money demanded by the ARA. Luis had told him that he and José had heard from local connections that Blackburn refused to pay the full *rescate* — the fee set by the guerrillas for the Mariposa gold mine site. Luis also said the people who lived on the river accused the multinational company of defrauding them of their property. In retaliation, the ARA would secure compensation for the local people through a kidnapped worker. Would Blackburn pay the guerrillas for a contracted-out driller when they wouldn't pay for the land? That depended upon company integrity, which left Will cold. If Blackburn wouldn't negotiate with the guerrillas on his behalf, and if T-Rex didn't have the cash, his time among the guerrillas would be very long indeed. The more time he spent in the jungle, the closer he came to being forgotten, and the less likely anyone would pay for his release.

El Capitán rarely spoke to Will. Whenever he did, it was to remind him of his motive for being in Colombia. "You and your Yankee friends are exploiting the Colombian people," he would say. "For five hundred years Colombia has been conquered, looted, and occupied by foreigners." Will was defenseless against the ghosts of Francisco Pizarro and Sebastián de Belalcazar, who had plundered the country in search of El Dorado. If Blackburn refused to pay, why would the guerrilla group keep him around? It was, in the end, all about the money.

The fifth day alone, he woke to the smell of coffee. His conscious state tugged at a dream of a quilt-covered Sunday morning spent cuddled up next to his wife. Theresa's skin smelled of rich, smoothly roasted coffee. Within seconds, his smiling wife faded and rematerialized as a guerrilla soldier named Jesús, hunched over a single-burner camp stove and picking his nose as he stirred granules of instant coffee into a plastic cup of water. "Jesus," moaned Will. He pulled his blanket over his head. "Jesus Christ!"

The sixth day alone, he sat in front of his tent admiring his sock and boot rack — four sticks jammed into the hillside. Now he could have dry footwear. He pulled the deck of cards, compliments of José, from his pocket. He sifted through them, shuffled, and played solitaire until dark.

The seventh day alone, Will sat in front of his tent and mended the hole in his socks with Fidel's needle and some string. A movement near El Capitán's tent made him look up from his darning. Ants. The last time he'd seen so many ants was in a tree fort in Yellowknife, papered with pictures torn out of a catalogue, of women posing in their underwear. The old poplar tree and its fort had been a haven for ants as well as boys reluctant to go home. But Yellowknife ants were Lilliputian compared to these brutes. Will watched as the ants merged into one solid mass that rippled up one side of El Capitán's tent and down the other. Will's scalp itched as he thought about the creatures flowing over blankets, through clothing, papers, maps, and books, tunnelling into El Capitán's pack, climbing up the tentpole and upside down across the ceiling. El Capitán would have to submit to this most communist of all armies, in which millions of individuals worked ceaselessly, fearlessly, and unquestioningly for the common good. The ants undulated past Will before splitting into long, narrow lines and disappearing into the surrounding shrubbery. Will knew they would return.

The eighth day alone, Will sat in front of his tent. He used his T-shirt to polish his boots. El Capitán's tent had relocated, and Will wondered if the commander had commiserated with a few lost and angry proletariats under his blanket during the night.

A Christmas-like atmosphere permeated camp with the arrival of new supplies. Will christened the pack animal the "yule mule." While the second-in-command distributed supplies, the soldiers seemed to have forgotten their lessons about material world corruption and succumbed to age-related behaviour. Will could see bags of rice and noodles, roundish fruits, flat tin cans, radios, Walkmans, a soccer ball (followed by a collective cheer), rolled-up newspapers, boxes of cigars and cigarettes, and a shiny aluminum cooking pot. Will was glad they hadn't found any army boots in his size yet. El Capitán continued to show his disdain for his yellow muckers. That's why he polished them.

Will noticed the second-in-command give Zhuri an envelope. She regarded the envelope, looked in his direction, and then slowly walked toward him with her rifle slung around her back. Most soldiers were simple people from the country, but Will saw a moneyed confidence and educated pride in her stride. Her young figure and pretty face invited fanciful male speculation. The closer she got, the more lovely and dangerous she became. Will looked up at her, framed by sunlight, and reminded himself that this girl was not much older than his own daughter. He invited her to sit down in front of his tent.

She removed her rifle and sat down beside him, her legs folded to one side. She gave him the envelope and began to twirl her long black braid in her fingers. She didn't wear her hair any other way. "It's for you, *Señor Eduardo,*" she said. Her "s" was a soft "th," indicating the Spanish of the privileged class.

As he accepted the muddied envelope, he held her eyes until she looked down at the letter. Will turned the already-opened envelope over in his big hands. Through the smudges, he saw his name in Theresa's handwriting. A photograph escaped from the envelope and fluttered between soldier and prisoner — Michael in his hockey equipment. Will picked up the picture and devoured it with his eyes. Michael leaned into the photo with a big grin on his face. Will grinned back. Thick shoulder pads gobbled up his neck and doubled his size. Will figured they'd fit better next year.

On the back of the hockey picture, in red pencil crayon, Michael had scrawled: "Hi Dad. I wish you were safe with Uncle Ted. I am getting better at sports." Drawn on the back of the picture were two figures wearing skates, one labelled "you" and the other "me." The picture spoke of winter afternoons and a thousand games of one-on-one hockey in front of the net in their driveway.

Absorbed in the photo, Zhuri moved closer to Will. Her arm touched his. He could feel the heat from the blackness of her hair and smell the forest of Colombia on her flawless skin. She asked him, "What is he wearing?"

"He's in his hockey equipment. You have to look big when you play hockey. It scares the other guy into giving you the puck."

"He looks like you," she said.

Will swallowed the lump in his throat. When he picked up the next photo, his heart melted. He smiled at the Grade Seven school picture of Kelly. Her complexion gleamed against a halo of jet-black hair — the same colour as his Cree mother's, whose hair remained black until the day she died. Why hadn't he noticed that Kelly's brown eyes were the same shape as Theresa's? On the back of her photo, in flowery script, Kelly had written: "Dear Dad, I wish that you were safe. I really miss you. I'm praying for you and your safe trip home. Love you always, Kelly." Coloured Xs and Os filled in all the white spaces.

"What's your daughter's name?"

"Kelly."

"How old is she?"

"Thirteen. Not a little girl anymore."

"She's pretty. She looks like a friend of mine from *Escuela Santa María Hortencia* — my Catholic girls' school. What's her school like?"

"It's a public school. Everyone in town goes to the same school — including boys."

"That would make school so much more fun. Does she have a boyfriend?"

"Maybe she does now. If I don't like him, I'll chase him away with a hockey stick," Will said with false bravado. He knew he had little control in that department.

His levity was lost on Zhuri. "That sounds like my father. He doesn't like my boyfriend." She dug into her pocket for the new package of cigarettes, courtesy of the yule mule, and a packet of matches.

"Oh, why not?"

"He's a guerrilla soldier."

"You're a guerrilla soldier. There must be another reason."

"I became a guerrilla soldier because Vicente joined. My father doesn't agree with the revolution, but if he ever talked to Vicente, he would realize they have a lot in common. But Father doesn't listen well. We had a big argument and I left home." She held her cigarette between her fingers; her hands fluttered with feminine grace.

"You left home for this? That must have been hard."

"Maybe for my father, but not for me. I don't think Father realized the depth of my conviction. Vicente and I are like Romeo and Julieta." She looked past the abandoned farmhouse. "Father always called him 'that boy from the *barrio*' instead of Vicente."

"Where is Vicente now?"

"I thought we would be together when I joined." Her voice faded into sadness. "Father wanted me to go to university, become some sort of professional, and forget Vicente."

"He probably wanted what was best for you. Do you like chasing mules, taking people hostage?"

"I want to marry Vicente." She pursed her lips and blew her smoke away from Will. "And I want to learn English. You have to know English for everything now, especially with computers. My brother has a restaurant in Bucaramanga — I could help him there while I finish school."

"That's a good plan. Your English will get a lot better in school than out here." As she tapped her cigarette, he reminded her, "Smoking is bad for you."

"Now you really sound like Father. He would say that if he knew."

Will's attention returned to his manhandled envelope. He fished out a wallet-sized family picture. Theresa's big brown eyes smiled at him. Whenever he thought of her, which was all the time, she was smiling. She looked so nice in that red jacket. He stood beside her. How could he stand that close to the woman he loved and not hold her? Kelly and Michael sat in front of him. God, he had the best kids in the world. He remembered when the picture was taken. It was the first snowfall of the year and Theresa wanted a family picture to send with Christmas cards. The photographer arranged their positions so that Theresa would not be taller than him. He didn't have to try to make them all smile.

Will saved the letter for the last. Apparently, the same muddied hand that had marred his envelope had scrutinized his letter. Theresa's writing reminded him of all the notes she left on the kitchen table for him: when to put the roast on, what to pick up at Overwaitea, what time Kelly's dance class was over....

Will read her words: "Dear Will, Everyone is praying for your safe return, no one more than me. I hope you keep your faith that we will all be together soon. Love you, Theresa."

He closed his eyes. He held the letter up to his nose to breathe in whatever traces of Theresa might still be clinging to it. The humidity had softened the paper so that it didn't crinkle against his whiskered cheek. He would have to shave off his whiskers before he rejoined his family, he thought. He wondered how that was ever going to happen now.

When he opened his eyes, Zhuri was still there. This time she held his gaze with her eyes. He could see that they too brimmed with tears because she had known the love of a family, and the pain of separation.

TWENTY

THE MIDNIGHT BUS TO BOGOTÁ was late, which gave the lovers time for a long, passionate farewell. Agustín missed her the minute she climbed aboard. As he walked along deserted streets back to the Hotel California, he wondered when he and Mercedes could stop saying goodbye to each other. He felt so empty without her. A cockroach the size of his little finger scuttled across the toe of his running shoe and under his door as he unlocked Room 222.

While he waited for his computer to jump to life, he thought about his sister Zhuri. He had hoped she would not be in the mountains with the guerrillas; it was dangerous and she was so naïve. Vicente, the guy she had run away with, wasn't even in the same resistance cell, so why was she still there? If he ever saw Vicente again, he would wring his revolutionary neck.

Agustín had two new emails. The message with the attached document from Vanessa had arrived at 12:33 AM. Mercedes had sent the other message yesterday before her arrival. Like a tasty *pastel de tres leches*, he would save her message for last. He clicked on Vanessa's message.

"Vanessa" was the code name for ARA headquarters and the voice that connected to Constanza's radio in the jungle. She was an unknown source in an unknown location that linked the war in the woods with the urban centres. Sometimes Vanessa wore the mantel of an old woman, sometimes the guise of a young man. A multitude of Vanessas flourished throughout rural Colombia. Via computer, she sent documents to Agustín for him to edit, translate, and forward to English-language publications in North America and Europe.

He opened the document, groaned at its length, and began to edit as he read. At times, Agustín had been disciplined by Vanessa for his edits. He had overworked certain documents and changed the flavour of the content. As he perused this document, he predicted further admonishment from Vanessa — it could not be sent without major restructuring. The paper's tone was incendiary. By page two, he could not continue.

Dios mío — who wrote this thing? Such a document would only increase hostility toward the movement and defeat its purpose — to garner financial support. He tipped back in his chair. This country surely boasted the longest-running unsuccessful guerrilla campaign in South America, and articles like this offered no solution to the decades of confrontation — no long-term goal, no new strategy. Nor would it give the ARA the respect it craved.

Agustín thought about the captured man. The more familiar he became with Nick and Ted, the more he saw the ARA through their eyes. The tools of the movement, kidnapping and extortion, were outdated. Sometimes hostages died. When this happened, the world beyond Colombia focused on results instead of the underlying causes.

And then there was the drug trade, which complicated everything in Colombia and blurred the line separating right from wrong.

Two years ago, before his life at Sebastian's, Agustín had lived in a university house filled with students passionately committed to change. Some even paid rent. Nights rang with idealistic political discussions and loud music. It was a world of black and white — after all, who could argue with "equality and justice for all"?

The document on the computer screen glared at him. Within its pages, Agustín saw a writer who had compromised ideals for power. Vitriol only encouraged negative reactions. Besides, thought Agustín, no one, no matter how politically sympathetic, would bother reading twelve pages of it.

Agustín longed for a country that welcomed the world, not one that made hostages of bird-watchers and company personnel who offered to train and provide jobs for Colombians. To invite people from other countries with different ideas, languages, customs, and foods would enrich his country. Tourism would revitalize the Hotel California. Uncle Oscar would love to see people dance the *cumbia* across its hardwood floors once again. But the Lonely Planet travel guides don't recommend Colombia. A drive in the country from the capital to the coast could cost you your freedom, or even your life. Colombia's mountains, its beaches, its incredible biodiversity, its people, and its history couldn't overcome the fact that tourists didn't travel to violent places.

Agustín could not complete his assignment.

He clicked onto the message from Mercedes. Since she quit the hotel and restaurant management program, Mercedes had thrown her energy into the "potshots and assassinations" business, the one retail business that was sure to thrive in a violent country: Bulletproof Clothing of Bogotá. Located in the heart of the business district, the shop promised high style and comfortable safety. The garments were all designed and sewn in Colombia, providing work for women in the outlying areas of the city. Clothing varied from pinstriped bulletproof suits to knife-repellent shirts, to leather or suede jackets with ballistic panels. Mercedes sold military clothing, de-mining suits and boots, as well as fashionable women's dresses and blazers. The clothing displayed in the storefront window rivaled that of any downtown department store. Most items were available in three levels of protection: nine-millimetre, .38, or Uzi.

The email made Agustín laugh. Upon her advice, the company installed a technical room, a.k.a. the "shooting gallery." Before buyers left the store, they could test the suit, vest, or blazer by standing in the path of a deadly projectile. Those who were shot were impressed, saying the bullet felt only like a small punch. Mercedes told him that leaders from Mexico, the U.S., and Greece, as well as a few aspiring African dictators, were lined up for the shopping experience.

Agustín thought about Mercedes. She couldn't get dough to rise, but she knew how to sell these modern-day suits of armour.

The clock on his dresser said 2:10 AM. In another four hours he'd be in the kitchen. Where was Zhuri when he needed her? He'd rewrite the document tomorrow. Then there was the call from the Secret Service. The last thing he wanted was trash like that sniffing around the Hotel California. He knew he should not leave this document on his computer, but his eyes refused to stay open. One more day shouldn't matter.

TWENTY-ONE

WHEN ALEJANDRO CRIED OUT, Will knew it was from pain. He and his two guards, Jenny and Juan, had orders to remain hidden by a stack of boulders so they could not come to Alejandro's aid. El Capitán and the other soldiers could not help, either. They had already crossed the exposed outcrop and were waiting in the forest on the other side at least a kilometre away. They could not hear the soldier's painful wail.

The snake at rest in the rocks may not have detected the vibration of Alejandro's approach. Without a warning, the viper uncoiled itself and struck the young soldier just above his boot. Alejandro cried out in painful surprise and crumpled as if whacked by a shovel. He dragged himself over the rocks back to the protective stack of boulders where Will and his two guards watched. Then he collapsed.

The guerrillas did not like to travel in the open or during the day when they were close to populated areas. However, Rosarito was just a small *pueblo*, and El Capitán did not have the luxury of time. He directed the second-in-command to lead Zhuri and the mule around the *pueblo* via a longer route, and ordered the others to cross the Rosarito basin. Caution was necessary because it was midday, and guerrilla scouts had reported seeing government soldiers in the town.

Open fields of artichokes grew throughout the basin next to fields of roses. The only irregularity in the geography was a boulder-strewn outcrop that skirted the basin's western edge. Forest remained intact on either side of the rock formation. El Capitán instructed the soldiers to sneak along the rock wall, one at a time, from one place of cover to the next. That way, if a sniper lay in wait, only one of them would die.

Jenny was a solid, muscular girl. She propped Alejandro up against his pack and laid his AK-47 next to him in the coarse grass. Will was not surprised at her ability to manhandle the wounded soldier. She ordered Juan to cross the rocky outcrop and find El Capitán. "*Rapido!*" Will saw that the young boy understood the danger and didn't need to be told to move quickly. Alejandro, fit and strong as he was, would not survive the afternoon without the antivenin in the commander's pack. As Juan bounded over the rocks, his forest camouflage clashed against the stone backdrop. Will wondered how many years he'd been a soldier, and how many more were ahead.

Suddenly, as if struck by a fist, Will realized the odds were even. For the first time in seventy-eight days, one captive faced one able soldier. Will had grown strong since his capture.

Jenny pulled some glossy, succulent leaves from a nearby plant. "Go and find me more of these," she ordered Will, displaying the collection cupped in her hand. Her callused hand belonged to someone who coaxed food to grow from the land, not the hand of a soldier. Alejandro shook with fever, tearing at his camouflage tunic. The girl unbuttoned it for him, and glared at Will. *"Ahora!* I need the leaves now! Leave your pack there."

Will dropped his pack where she pointed and foraged for the needed plants.

She ripped a shirt from her pack into strips as he emptied his cap full of leaves next to her. *"Más!"* She wanted more. Will watched her break open the thick leaves and squeeze the juice onto a strip of cloth. Alejandro rolled from side to side, clutching at his leg. His eyes were wild with delirium.

"Calmate, lie still, lie still. Try to be calm." She spoke comfortingly to Alejandro while she pressed fluid from the leaves into the cloth until it dripped green serum. "Roll up his pantleg. I need both my hands." Will felt the soldier's heat as he loosened his boot and eased the pantleg past two perfect puncture wounds surrounded by discoloured skin. Will leaned into the patient to hold him steady while Jenny wrapped the poultice above the reddish streak that ran up his leg. She was close enough that Will could have placed both his hands around her neck.

"Have you got water?" she asked, looking at his pack. He did. He pulled out his canteen. In front of him, her rifle leaned lifelessly against her pack. It was an M-16, a more lightweight model than Alejandro's AK-47. Will recalled the time when he and a friend from Maracaibo went target shooting with the same Venezuelan-made rife. It fired about eight hundred rounds a minute. He looked at the girl's back and concentrated on controlling his breathing as she tended her patient.

He passed his canteen to her. She doused one of the rags with water and placed it against Alejandro's lips so he could suck the moisture from it. She draped a second wet cloth on his forehead.

Will crouched an arm's length away from the gun. He estimated that he had less than fifteen minutes until Juan returned with El Capitán. He could use a fifteen-minute lead.

If he didn't pick up her gun, he could remain a hostage in the jungle... possibly for years. Some time ago, they passed a second guerrilla group with a prisoner in tow. The man's hands were bound and a rope had been slung around his neck. But it was the man's eyes that haunted Will at night. Downcast, vacant eyes told a story of a man who had lost hope.

Will remembered Luis' words: "Every day without freedom is too long." Every day Will hoped for a chance like this. He was just as insane as the last prisoner if he thought any money might appear on his behalf. If Blackburn paid the ransom, the company could lose every gold mine it held in Colombia. The Colombian government did not favour companies that submitted to guerrilla demand.

If he did pick up the gun, he would have to kill her. And the snake-bitten soldier. Possibly the boy soldier and the commander, too.

The female soldier gave Alejandro another drink. She held his hand and talked soothingly to him, gently shushing him, trying to slow the movement of blood through his body.

Will would have to move fast. Now was the time.

When she turned toward him, he saw the alarm in her expression. Her mouth opened and he heard the quick intake of breath. Colour drained from her wide, unlined face. She would have to reach past the prisoner for her gun. In that moment, she knew she had failed as a soldier. Will looked into her brown eyes, filled with the knowledge of her impending death.

Now. He would lean over and pick up the gun. He would fire it into her soldier's chest. Blood would splatter him and the injured man because they were so close to one another. He would steal the clip from her belt and run before the others arrived. He would run back along the path, veer uphill through thick and viny undergrowth. Uphill. He had prepared for this moment since the day Zhuri chased the runaway mule. He would run until he reached the Arauca River that divided Colombia and Venezuela. He'd run and run and run and no one would catch him. He would be a free man.

"Now!" the voice in his head screamed.

In the silence of the afternoon, an orange speckled butterfly fluttered between the soldier and the prisoner. It alit, opening and closing its wings, upon the steel barrel of the M-16, where Will and Jenny's gazes met.

The moment was gone.

Will turned away. This country was awash in useless killings. His Norwegian father told him that there were no unwounded soldiers in war. Will could not kill the young soldiers.

Both soldier and prisoner heard the crunch of hard-soled boots against rolling stones. El Capitán hurried past the snake's vacant ledge and around the stack of boulders until he stood before the captive, the kneeling girl soldier, and the prone soldier. Juan followed — the boy soldier who looked very much like Michael, Will's own son.

TWENTY-TWO

TOO LARGE TO STAND UP STRAIGHT, the heads of giant sunflowers drooped heavily over the crowd below. Theresa and Niyal perused the displays showcasing the very best of the Monarch Valley fields, farms, and gardens for 1998. Bright red vine-ripened tomatoes, meticulously canned peaches, and sheaves of husked and bearded grains filled tables crowded together the entire length of the recreation centre. For one hundred years, the Monarch Valley Fall Fair had celebrated the harvest and given the people of the valley a sense of pride and a place to meet. Everyone stopped to ask Theresa about Will, shake their heads sympathetically, and to "call them if there was anything they could do." Theresa smiled in return and hoped the cracks in her mental state didn't show. The blackened kitchen calendar told the family that September 9 was Will's seventy-eighth day in captivity.

Yesterday's interview with Bjorn at the *Monarch Valley Press* had gone well. He showed a sensitivity and true concern for her feelings. The article would appear in next Thursday's paper.

Within the hallways of Monarch Valley High, Kelly suffered more downs than ups. She told her mom that Grade Eight sucked. One-time friends talked about her behind her back. She didn't "get" math, and Kat shared more classes with Julia than with her. And she had four new zits.

In Mr. Mason's Grade Four class, Michael fidgeted at his desk. He could hardly wait for his turn at show and tell. Folded in his pocket was the letter from his dad. Michael didn't even have to read it — he had memorized every word.

— — —

It was a Tuesday night. The kids were in bed and the home computer was hers. Theresa looked at the screen. Where it said "number of copies," she typed in "45." Forty-five letters would soon land on forty-five desks of forty-five Members of Parliament. If she could spark an interest in her plight, Foreign Affairs might receive forty-five phone calls. That might cause someone in the ministry to try a new tactic... find a loophole... talk to someone who knew... forge a new policy... make a deal... and find some way to retrieve her husband.

Last night's conversation with Foreign Affairs ended with bad feelings on both sides. Theresa lost her patience defending Nick again. Jim Itch's replacement — Theresa didn't care enough to remember her name — accused Nick of playing Rambo. What was he doing talking to the guerrillas? The government was clearly frustrated with Nick and reminded Theresa that capitulating to terrorist demands would only encourage them to kidnap more workers. Theresa told her that Nick talked to the guerrillas because he cared about Will.

"You don't know how close we are to getting this solved," the replacement woman snapped at her. "If Nick goes into the ARA camp and something happens, it'll be on your head."

That stung. What had Foreign Affairs done for her family? They never gave her any information that she hadn't given them first, and they seemed more connected to Blackburn than to her. "Let's be real," Theresa said. "We're dealing with a corrupt country here. This situation is beyond the control of the Colombian government and even if it did intervene, there's a big chance that things could get worse. C'mon. Grease the right palms — there's got to be something you can do."

Nick had met with the guerrillas twice and agreed to meet again. It was Nick who received Will's letter. It was Nick who faxed the letter to Theresa at the optometry clinic. Will's letter was the only proof of life Theresa ever received. At least he had been alive when he wrote the letter. How could this woman with her telephone headset know what that meant to her and the kids? Theresa supposed she shouldn't have slammed the phone down, but she didn't want this unfeeling official to know she was crying. She licked the final stamp and planted a kiss on the last envelope. Maybe one out of the forty-five MPs would have the faceless bitch fired.

Nick told her the ARA wanted $2 million US for Will's freedom. Well, that was down from the original six. But holy shit, she thought, the figure was still beyond her means. She arranged a date with Jerry, her real estate friend, to discuss mortgaging the house. She would go apartment hunting on Saturday, despite Kelly's protestations of "I'm not living in any crappy apartment!" What was the alternative? Her family was not the first to discover that freedom had its price.

Theresa searched the Internet for Canadian mining companies until she found Blackburn Resources International.

Nice, she said to herself. *Obviously they have money to spend on their website.* She looked at pictures of workmen in mountainous terrain wearing hard hats and knee-high yellow work boots. She scrolled down the list of executives until she found a name she liked: Steve Steel. She would call Mr. Steel and ask what time he would meet with her at the company headquarters in downtown Vancouver. This week would be more convenient for her than next week. She would be armed with the phone number of a particularly persistent journalist from the *Ottawa Citizen.*

Most people who knew Theresa would not describe her as threatening, aggressive, or impatient. But after seventy-eight days, Theresa discovered that a bitchy attitude can be quite effective. In fact, forcing something to happen felt good, and she hadn't felt good since that last long hug at Spokane International Airport.

TWENTY-THREE

THE BOTTLE OF WHISKEY LEANED AGAINST WILL like a sleeping friend. He sat in front of his tent in the early afternoon, writing in his diary. This was odd because Will usually wrote his notes after dark, away from the watchful eye of El Capitán. Today he had plans for after dark and it involved his sleeping friend. He wrote: "September 12. Day 81. Bottle of whiskey. Merry Christmas."

Christmas arrived before lunch. In the tradition of jolly old St. Nick, the yule mule brought something for everyone. Once the fresh supplies were stowed away and the mule loaded with sacks of coffee beans for the return trip, all the soldiers plugged new cassettes and batteries into old players and vanished from view. Except Francisco.

Displaying even more teeth than the yawning mule, Francisco sauntered toward Will, hands hidden behind his back. Still no size twelve army boots. Francisco presented Will with a bottle of Colombian whiskey. Unopened. Will regarded his gift with surprise and puzzlement. Why would they give him this? He offered to share the contents, but Francisco grinned even wider, shook his head, and said, "You deserve it, man," and walked away.

Before he opened the bottle, Will thumbed through his diary. "September 11. Day 80. Picked coffee beans with soldiers. September 9. Day 78. Killed coral snake." Aha, he thought. Maybe this explained the bottle of whiskey.

Will and some of the soldiers had gathered under the kitchen tarp, loitering, while Angela prepared the midday meal. When she reached up into the food storage tree for the bananas, a red and black banded coral snake dropped in front of her. She screamed and jumped backward, tipping over the pot of cooked rice. Shaken from its repose, the snake wriggled one way and then another before darting toward Alejandro and Francisco. The boys galloped away in opposite directions, Alejandro still limping from his last snake encounter. Will leaned on his staff passively until the metre-long snake twisted toward him. With one well-aimed blow, he killed the venomous reptile with his walking stick and flung it to the edge of the clearing. The soldiers, impressed by Will's coolness, jostled each other for the best view of the dead snake.

Will turned to another page in his diary. "September 7. Day 76. Caught Miguel cheating." Card games may have been the apex of conceptual thought for many of the soldiers. All six soldier boys — Francisco, Alejandro, Jesús, Fidel, Miguel, and even young Juan — liked to play rummy with Will, but only three could play at a time. Will ruled that when one of them lost, he had to drop out so another could play. Nobody wanted to lose. When Will caught Miguel cheating, he hit the boy's hand with his staff. Miguel jumped up, inflamed by the assault on his machismo and grabbed his rifle. Francisco and Fidel had to persuade him to put the gun down so the game could continue. Will, unfazed by a cocked Kalashnikov inches from his nose, warned Miguel on the next deal, "You can't cheat a Canadian."

— — —

The memory of September 3, Day 72, made him salivate. "Wild pig for supper." He could almost taste the grease that ran down his chin. The poor little pig was doomed the second it wandered into camp. The ensuing hunt transcended boundaries of age, rank, nationality, captor, and captive. Will took his turn with the other males as they tried to tackle the squealing beast. They would not risk the sound of a rifle. It was Jesús who trapped the animal under his body and slit its throat as quickly as he would open a bag of tortilla chips. Will winced. The act of killing had been frighteningly easy for him.

Blank page. "August 19. Day 57. Michael's birthday." Blank page. Blank page.

Will tucked his pencil and diary into his coveralls pocket, and screwed the cap off his whiskey. He breathed in the acrid smell of a country at war with itself. A war that he was now a part of. Will was aware that the present stalemate could not go on forever. Sometimes rules get broken in wartime and sometimes people who aren't supposed to get killed, get killed. He breathed the fumes once again — this time detecting a slight improvement — and wondered what El Capitán would do with him. The whiskey was a poor substitute for freedom, but it would help him forget that tomorrow would be day 82.

Will passed out before sundown — in front of his tent with his yellow boots on.

— — —

The yule mule had not forgotten El Capitán. Secretly elated, Frederico Constanza retired to a hammock across the creek from camp with his newspaper and a box of Cuban cigars. In the quiet afternoon, Constanza brought a Cohiba up to his nose and inhaled deeply. *Ahh* — the aroma of a tiny island revolution. An armed uprising that had outlasted ten American presidents and twice as many CIA directors.

Spitting distance from the Florida coast, Cuba had put Washington on a collision course with most of Latin America and reminded the world that the United States of America could be beaten.

Constanza unrolled his Cuban newspaper. Spread across the front page of *El Granma* was Fidel Castro, survivor of six hundred failed assassination attempts, addressing an attentive Havana crowd. The printed transcript of the speech took up the entire first section of the newspaper.

The smell of the newspaper carried Constanza back to his childhood. He remembered being part of a large crowd, listening to the passionate deliberations of Colombia's defender of the oppressed, Camilo Torres. Unable to recall words, young Frederico felt the adoration of the people surrounding the man. Speeches in the plaza didn't end when the crowd dispersed; they continued at his family's house, all night long. Many a time, Frederico and his brother had given up their beds to strangers with unfamiliar accents. The boys would sleep in the cellar, where the smell of freshly printed newspapers stacked on the hand-cranked copier overpowered the smell of earthen walls and stored vegetables. Amid the turmoil of voices and shuffling feet, beams of light shone down on them through the cracks in the wooden floor.

When the Colombian army murdered Torres in 1966, people poured into the streets of Bogotá to mourn the loss. Through his death, Torres breathed fire into the minds of many young people. Just as Torres had cast off his Catholic robes to join the revolution, the Constanza brothers embraced the Arauca Revolutionary Army, believing only armed struggle could change the present power structure. They dedicated their lives to the future socialist state of Colombia.

Constanza relied on *El Granma* for inspiration. But today, he could not concentrate. He read the same paragraph five times, his mind wandering from the page to thoughts of the meeting in progress between Simón Bolívar Juárez, his second-in-command, and the Canadian hostage mediator. Constanza had ordered Fidel and Miguel to accompany Simón to the third meeting with Nick and Alonso.

Constanza disliked the hostage situation. Simón's report from previous meetings corresponded with reports from central headquarters and from their urban contact in Bucaramanga. Their hostage, this Will Edwards, was a working-class man — no credentials, no initials behind his name, no six-figure salary. The ARA would have to drop its price. Again.

Frederico Constanza sighed as he folded his newspaper neatly for Simón. He yawned. Were they any closer to their socialist state than Torres had been? Constanza was nearing fifty. He had seen the armed conflict change from one of political ideals to one for control over natural resources, coca farm management, and land. Slimy dealers proliferated and drug money financed more and more of the ARA's operations. Every year he lost a little more passion, and every year his sciatica worsened — a constant, miserable, nagging *dolor en la nalga*.

Prior to this hostage-taking, Constanza had urged the ARA to take a more proactive role in bargaining with the mining company over the Mariposa so they could channel a percentage of the mine's profits into local villages. But those talks fizzled because the multinational company refused to bargain in good faith. Why was he not surprised when the company reneged on their unwritten contract? He'd better damned well get something for this Canadian.

Constanza looked across the creek into camp. His supposed "Blackburn executive" lay sprawled out and snoring in front of his tent. And fuck those yellow boots! Will Edwards was taking up too much of his time. Things would have to change soon. He had instructed Simón to pass that message on to Nick.

TWENTY-FOUR

MONEY MOVED. Five-hundred-dollar chips clacked against thousand-dollar chips. Slot machines dinged, clanged, and spat coins down metal chutes into eager buckets. A roulette wheel mounted on a black walnut table clicked into place. Alabaster pillars supported a ceiling dripping with crystal chandeliers. Inspired by the excesses of Monaco, the Crystal Casino on the forty-acre private island of the Renaissance Aruba Resort lacked nothing but clocks.

If Nick cared, he would have noticed that his rumpled appearance clashed with that of the resident glitterati. His dark hair was disheveled, and his razor was back in Bucaramanga. His leather jacket, pocked with cigarette burns, barely reached his jeans, which smelled of diesel fuel. It was not his casual attire, though, so much as his determined look that set him apart from the rest of the casino's waxen clientele.

Charles Welshley Blackburn enjoyed the Dutch colony's white sand beaches, its aromatic cigars, its high-class escort services, and its opulent casinos. It was where he did his banking and where he liked to play. With an economy driven by gold, oil, offshore banking, and tourism, there were few poor people to disturb his good mood.

Acting on a tip, Nick found Blackburn in a full tuxedo with an empty martini glass in hand. The ruffle over his stomach bumped against the bucket of coins clutched in the crook of his elbow. He stood at the rail as a horse race thundered across an enormous television screen. With eyes fixed on the bay surging for the finish line, Blackburn enunciated every word: "He's not my man, Nick." When the race ended, he added, "I have said that so many times that even a driller as dense as the Canadian Shield should be able to understand."

Nick followed the burly man from the rail to the nearest slot machine. "Hello, Mr. Blackburn," he said. "Let's not forget basic South American courtesy." Blackburn ignored Nick's extended hand. Instead, he pulled a coin from his bucket, plugged it into the machine, and pulled the handle. *Flip. Flip. Flip flip flip.* Another coin. Another pull. Nick concentrated on Blackburn's pasty face, not the pull of the machine. His old gambling habits were not entirely behind him. Blackburn concentrated on the spinning wheels.

"Do you know what it's called when someone demands money from you to bolster their own illegal activities? It's called extortion. I'm not giving those Commie bastards one more fat peso, loonie, quetzal, dollar, bloody rooster, or pretty-coloured shell. You know damn well that if I pay extortion fees to guerrillas, it would jeopardize our official exploration and property rights. How many people do you think that would put out of work?" Blackburn finally looked at Nick. "I've got a very nice grouping of gold and silver mines that I don't intend to forfeit. And besides," he added, "it's the law."

Nick snorted. "Since when have you become so law-abiding? Payin' vaccines to rebel groups is against the law, too. Seems to me you've been doin' a bit of that for years, except this year you thought you could cut them a little short."

"So sue me." Blackburn turned his attention back to the machine as he pulled the handle again. Two men in black suits with shiny black hair appeared, as if emerging from neighbouring slot machines. They casually stood on either side of Nick, about an arm's length behind him.

"Look, Chuck, you know, I know, Will knows — he's the kidnapped guy, by the way — the workers know, *everyone* knows you fucked up. Security issues were all supposed to be managed through Blackburn Resources International. I hired my guys because I trusted you. I passed that assurance onto my men. I wouldn't have asked them down here if those details were not tended to. My reputation is at stake here, and so, by God, is yours. You've got a responsibility to get that man outta the jungle before he rots."

Blackburn stopped feeding the machine. "I don't appreciate people I hire to do a simple job telling me what I can or can't do. And don't call me 'Chuck.' Diamond drillers are a dime a dozen. I can get six replacements at the stage bar, including the painted whore, and have them trained by the time the moon comes up over Miami."

"That's not the point. You know fuckin' well what I'm talking about. Unless you get involved, you'll never get another worker to set foot on anything that smells like Blackburn in all of South America. How are you gonna run your operation without workers?"

"It wasn't my idea to close the mine." Blackburn motioned to one of the men for a cigarette. The man in black on Nick's left reached into his suit jacket, stepped closer to Blackburn, and presented one to him. He backed into his former position while the man on Nick's right flicked a gilded lighter. Smoke clouded Nick's airspace.

He moved closer to Blackburn. "The mining community is a small town," he said. "Word travels fast. Guys aren't gonna go back to a place without any protection. And another thing: not goin' to work is their way of sayin' that Will mattered to them. Remember Will, the guy that got fuckin' kidnapped? Some of the local guys are hurtin' right now without a job to go to."

"Local guys are not my concern, Nick. If I'm going to get all wet and soggy over some local village people or their dog that I ran over, I may as well fold up my tent and business license and see if I can go volunteer for the Red Cross. This whole goddamn charade is making business very undoable in that derelict of a country. If El Presidente catches me doing what you're trying to guilt me into doing, he can freeze the assets of the company and the whole royal Blackburn family." He turned his attention back to the slots.

"Don't lecture me about reputation. I've sunk a shitload of money into the Mariposa to bring that place out of the dark ages. I've hired experienced people to get a top-quality job done. The machines and the equipment and the whole goddamned work camp rank above standard. And I've spent a gold mine on bribes." Blackburn hardly glanced at the slot machine before plugging in another coin. "If you want him out, you pay. Everyone is on the take, especially your Commie jungle friends. I just do what everyone does. I take what's mine, then I get the hell outta Dodge." *Flip flip flip.*

Begging for money sickened him, but Nick needed cash. His mouth was dry; the gambling machines called his name. The cologne-drenched guys in suits standing too close made him nervous. He couldn't leave without some kind of commitment from Blackburn. He'd beg if he had to. In a more conciliatory tone, he said, "I wouldn't be here unless I had to be. It's been ninety days. Somethin's gonna crack soon. Will is a helluva good foreman. Learned the drillin' business at the good ol'-fashioned school of hard knocks. Never gives you any grief, and always gets the job done." Nick reached for his own cigarette and tapped it in his hand. "I need a million bucks."

Blackburn laughed. "Give it up, Nick. Blackburn Resources

International didn't get to be a big operation by supporting movements dedicated to destroying business-friendly governments. Me and Uncle Sam want to keep it that way. Do you see what's happening next door in Venezuela?"

"I'm not supportin' anyone in this war. I'm tryin' to get a guy home. A guy I hired. A guy with a family waiting for my next phone call. That's what I support. If we don't believe in that, what in hell do we believe in?"

Blackburn hardened. "Son of a bitch! I've got my own debts that aren't getting paid. Arsenic-laden sludge leaked into a river in the Philippines, *allegedly*, and some bullshit Mining Watch group of do-gooders high on homegrown is dogging my ass about it. I've got the Mariposa on hold while the Commie bastards screw me, my wife's lawyer just dinged me for another ten grand — I hope the bastard likes quarters — and you want me to pity some ugly driller and give you *how* much money? If I were handing out cash in that goddamn drug-infested country, I'd hand it to El Presidente for a big new helicopter so he could fly over those bastards and drop something that goes boom. I'm this close" — he pinched his fingers together in front of Nick's face — "to hiring my own paramilitary marching band to really fuck those Commie bastards." Blackburn's face was as red as if he'd just run the five hundred. He gripped the handle on the slot machine with extra vigour and pulled down hard. Nick felt a hand tighten around each of his elbows.

Blackburn composed himself and smoothed his ruffled shirt. The men behind Nick let go of his arms. In a calm voice, Blackburn added, "From where I stand, I see an empty chair at a card table. I also see a sweet handful of cards that's going to take care of my next ex-wife's payment." He handed Nick his bucket of coins and said, "Take this. Go and win yourself some Commie dough. If that doesn't work, give me a call in a few days. I could use that D-8 caterpillar of yours on some coal beds I've got my eye on. If you're selling, talk to

Hector." He wrote Hector's number on a Crystal Casino coaster with a gold pen from his breast pocket.

Blackburn undid another button on his shirt, revealing two more loops of gold chain. Accompanied by the men in black, he entered the smoky glass room where the players had more diamonds on their hands than calluses. Nick stood alone at the slots with a full bucket of silver coins. He stopped a cocktail waitress and exchanged the bucket for two glasses of dark rum on her tray. Places like this made him thirsty. Then he walked out the door of the casino into the humid Aruba night and lit his cigarette.

— — —

Nick paid the airline worker at the ticket counter of the Queen Beatrix International Airport an extra fifty dollars to get him on the next flight to Maracaibo, Venezuela. It was garage sale time. He planned to visit some friends in the drilling business and discuss inventory. He'd already committed Hector's number to memory.

TWENTY-FIVE

FREEDOM — OR WAS IT? El Capitán called it an exchange.

Will suspected that his brother had arranged a payoff. What other kind of exchange would he mean? Surely not an exchange of people. He couldn't stand the thought of gaining freedom at his brother's expense. He placed his boots in Francisco's footsteps over the uneven terrain beside the waterfall. With confused energy, he clutched at branches and hoisted himself up the slippery incline. They'd been slogging their way up to Mosquito Camp since yesterday and Francisco said they planned to be there by nightfall. Two months ago, Luis and José had been released from the Mosquito Camp location. Today was September 25. Will had been a prisoner for ninety-four days and was ready to go home. He had had enough of the rocks and trees of Colombia. And he'd definitely had enough rice and beans and canned sardines.

About three-quarters of the way up the mountain, just below the persistent cloud cover, they found the camp hidden in a forest of bamboo. It was nearly dark when the cloud of bloodsucking insects welcomed the group back to the familiar bench of land. From the way he was puffing, Will estimated the elevation to be around ten thousand feet. He sat down to catch his breath and watch the soldiers set up the tents and raise the tarp over the kitchen area where the stove and food supplies had been dropped. He also noticed the darkening sky and the soldiers pulling on layers of clothing as the temperature fell. Because of the rush to get camp set up before the rain and a total blackout, they went to bed hungry.

Will lay on his groundsheet listening to the rain on his tent, anticipating freedom. The rain began as a patter, but quickly turned into a downpour. There must be as many names for rain in this country as the Inuit have for snow, Will mused. He remembered the Amazon rainstick he'd found for Kelly on a previous job in Peru. It was a hollow branch filled with seeds that spoke the language of the rainforest when tipped on its end. The toy sounded very real in their living room in Monarch Valley. But not here. Rivulets of water raced toward him from the open space between the tent canopy and the ground. He wrapped his groundsheet around his lower half as the rain poured implacably down around him. Will thought of the mudslide on his first day of captivity, and wondered how any of the mountain roads could remain passable in a climate of such extreme precipitation.

Then he dared to think about going home. He had refused to allow his mind to go there until he was certain his release was imminent. No, not yet. He'd think about home once he had his seat belt on and his tray table up.

— — —

The next day, the weather was unsettled. Several times throughout the day, El Capitán and the second-in-command disappeared into the forest with the field radio. Each time they left, Will expected them to return and tell him where to leave his army gear and show him the way home. The soldiers spent the day building up their beds so they wouldn't get wet at night. It looked like another storm was on its way.

Will paced as the day wound down and the wind picked up. It relieved the camp of mosquitoes but contributed to Will's agitation. Where was El Capitán? What in hell was going on? Surely they weren't playing with his head, taunting him with freedom? It occurred to Will that they could be lying to him. What better way to keep someone from planning escape?

Will's watch read 4:15 PM by the time El Capitán and the second-in-command returned to camp. They addressed the soldiers. In competition with the wind, and with ears dulled from years of heavy machinery, Will saw El Capitán mouth the words he could not and did not want to hear. They would return to Camp Coffee at daybreak.

Will boiled inside — all of El Capitán's freedom talk was just bullshit. His ability to hide emotion made him a good cardplayer, but a difficult man to reason with. Whenever Theresa wanted to talk out a problem, he clammed up. It was not his way to express his feelings through words. Will retreated to his tent, his jaw set — there was no way in hell he would return to Camp Coffee. If they wouldn't give him freedom, he would goddamned well take it. Tonight. The oncoming storm would be his ticket to freedom.

Darkness dropped like the slamming of a prison door. The wind shrieked and turned the surrounding bamboo into a forest of whips. It ripped the nylon tarp off the camp supplies and sent dried foodstuff and the aluminum pot flying. Will tightened his tent's guy ropes and gave the pegs an extra push with his foot before he ducked inside. The canvas walls shook with such ferocity that a train could have passed by without him noticing. Above him, the thunder and lightning were simultaneous. Through the tent flaps, Will could see the camp, the sky, the forest, and the soldiers bent double in the blue light, scurrying to gather all the scattered goods. There was so much electricity in the air, Will felt the hair on his forearms stand on end.

When the rain began, it crashed down with even more might and fury than the night before. Will felt he was inside a waterfall. The last time he witnessed such a deluge, he had just batted in the winning run for the Coffin Dodgers. It was May, the sun had been hot, and Theresa's nose was sunburned. When he reached the dugout, a teammate tipped the cooler of cold water over him. Theresa laughed and the kids cheered from the stands. Joyous thoughts of his family solidified his need to escape. It was more powerful than the rain beating against his tent and deeper than the pain in his joints. He drew a map of his escape route in his mind. The Arauca River couldn't be more than a night and a day's bushwhacking away.

Lightning illuminated his watch. He would leave for Venezuela after the next shift change. That would give him six hours of darkness ahead of his captors. Will planned to exit through the back flap of his tent. He would climb to the top of the mountain, into the cloud forest, and follow the height of land to the valley of the Arauca. To cross the river, he could tie the legs of his coveralls together and puff air into them for floatation. When he reached Venezuela, he would find the drilling site he helped set up three years ago, and the foreman, Julian Hernández. Big Julie would get him home.

His escape plan contained a lot of maybes, and his mental map had no scale. If he fell and injured himself, he'd be torn apart by predators long before the soldiers found him. Or he could stay and watch his strength and sanity leave his body as surely as a bad smell. He pressed the button that shone an aqua light on his watch. The guard would change within the hour.

Will had to strain to hear the sound of Alejandro's limp exchanging places with Zhuri's light step. An hour passed; the storm softened to a steady rainfall. Will quietly packed his belongings and rolled his groundsheet into his knapsack, a manoeuvre he had practiced many times. He checked on his guard again. Zhuri sat on the wet ground hugging her knees. Her head rested on her crossed arms. Was she asleep? If she was, that would make his escape so much easier. He looked out again. This time he noticed that her thin poncho did not protect her from the bamboo that bent down, water pouring off the branches like running faucets. Will remembered she had given up her groundsheet to cover the gear that would not fit under the kitchen tarp earlier this afternoon. She shivered so feverishly that Will wondered if she had malaria. He waited a few more minutes inside his tent. Something wasn't right. Then he heard her sob.

"Christ," Will muttered as he sat back on his knees, anticipating the next sob. There it was. One after another after another. Just like when his daughter cried after a bad dream. His head fell into his hands. He massaged his brow, took off his glasses and wiped the splatters onto his damp shirt, then put his glasses back on. He wanted to put his fist through the tent wall. Why couldn't he just walk away? It wasn't his misery; she wasn't his daughter. This was not his war. "Goddamn it all to hell," he said as he looked out the back tent flap at the soaking-wet, beckoning free world. He unpacked his groundsheet and crawled out the front flap. He placed his groundsheet down for her to sit on and sat beside her. With his jacket held over their heads, she leaned into him and released a flood of tears. She shook so much he put his arm around her and held her the same way he had held his own children. They held onto each other, finding warmth in the touch of another human being. He felt her thin shoulders heaving through her wet poncho and gave out a great, long sigh.

His escape plan was caught in the same current as the beetles swirled away by the torrents of rain. But then, in Colombia, many plans were washed away. Plans like running away with your soldier boyfriend to show your father that you can make your own decisions. Plans to kidnap a rich foreign capitalist for money. Plans to live a peaceful life in a country where basic human rights are not a given. Resigned to his present reality, and his lost opportunity, Will held the girl until her shaking subsided.

An image of Theresa in her red jacket materialized before him. He lifted his arm to feel her face. The ethereal form reached out her arms toward him. She didn't want him to throw his life away into the wet, dark night. He absorbed her eyes, her lips, her welcoming arms. She helped him to understand that El Capitán was not messing with his head — something had gone wrong. He was at this location for a reason. Someone on the outside was negotiating for his release. He just had to wait it out. Will looked at Zhuri and pitied her, but this was not where he should be. He left his groundsheet and his jacket with her, and crawled back into his tent, and collapsed on the wet ground. He could not leave for freedom without his jacket.

— — —

Days later, a war between fever and chills raged within his body. Will sat cross-legged in front of his tent, his hands folded, overlooking the coffee plantation. His black hair, stiff with grime, nearly reached his shoulders. He had no appetite, and his gut ached. His pants didn't fit him anymore. Large blisters that looked like second-degree burns had broken out on his neck. He scratched his mosquito bites until they bled. At Mosquito Camp, he had given his watch to Zhuri. Francisco had his cards. The soldier boys continued their games without him. He declined their invitations.

Two blue butterflies danced past his eyes, interrupting his thoughts. A metallic blue iridescence flashed on and off as they flew. He stared at them, hypnotized, as they fluttered past the card-players and skipped apart, following their zigzagging, seemingly random path into the coffee bushes. What would it feel like to be free?

Suddenly, the sky darkened, but Will didn't notice because his hands started to tingle. He opened and closed his fingers. The sensation moved up his arms, into his body, and down his legs. He felt light-headed and light-bodied at the same time — as if he were float-ing. He rose above the camp, above the cardplayers, who paid him no attention, and above the coffee bushes where the butterflies played. Will looked in awe at an expansive, soundless blue-green vista. A breeze brushed his skin and tousled his hair. He was flying. It was exhilarating. He knew he was flying over Colombia because on his left, he could see the Pacific Ocean kissing the curve of the conti-nental shore. To his right were mountains wrapped in green as soft as the fur of an animal. He was flying north — north to freedom, to Canada, to his family. Slowly, he turned his head. Where his out-stretched arms had once been, wings now sprouted from his back. They gleamed a metallic blue, the colour of freedom.

TWENTY-SIX

THE RED LIGHT below the video camera blinked on as Theresa and Diamond Joe Jessup entered the boardroom on the thirty-second floor of a West Georgia Street office tower in Vancouver. Steve Steel leaned back in his chair, his arms stretched behind his head and his legs apart. Two more Blackburn executives, accompanied by two lawyers, swivelled their high-backed leather chairs to face the newcomers.

Without any attempt to set his guests at ease, Steve stood and introduced himself and the other men encircling the rosewood table. Theresa felt intimidated and grievously unprepared; she immediately forgot every one of the names. Diamond Joe introduced himself. There were no handshakes. Months ago, when he learned about Will being taken hostage, Diamond Joe had offered his expertise to Theresa. He and Will were good friends and had worked together back when mining was more fashionable in B.C. Theresa took advantage of his offer once the meeting date with Blackburn had been set.

Diamond Joe spoke first. He reminded all at the table that it was nearly October and Will had been a captive of the ARA for three months. He then introduced Theresa. She took a big breath of indoor air and directed her question toward Steve: "I came here to find out what Blackburn Resources International has done to get Will out of Colombia."

Steve was well suited for this urban altitude. He calmly assured her that he and the Blackburn team were concerned about Will and were working closely with Foreign Affairs. In the same patronizing tone Jim Litchfield had used, expertly moved the agenda from hers to his. Begrudgingly, Theresa had to admire his gift — he was a natural politician.

She looked past Steve through the floor-to-ceiling windows. How perfect the city appeared from so high up. Colourful toy cars zipped noiselessly along treed boulevards arranged in unblemished order. Beyond the green expanse of Stanley Park, where the ocean met the land, ominous clouds gathered and began to barrel toward the office tower. Within seconds, a hard rain slammed against the window.

Tears welled up in Theresa's eyes when she realized the futility of this meeting. No matter what happened outside the room, people inside would remain unaffected. Before Steve called it a wrap, Theresa asked if she could say something. She swallowed the quiver in her voice, and focussed on Steve. "You've told me what you've done," she said. "I want to know what you are going to do."

His look said, "What didn't you get the first time?" But what he said out loud was, "What do you mean?"

"You paid $8,000 the last time a worker was kidnapped." The executive nearest the door coughed, but Theresa continued. "I mean, if there is a ransom, what will you pay now?"

"What is the ransom?"

Diamond Joe interjected. "Everyone in this room knows that $2 million US is more than this family can afford. They want to know how much you will pay."

Steve coolly replied, "We will pay anything that is reasonable."

"And what would that be?"

"Indirectly, we are paying right now, as we are in the midst of a delicate negotiation. Government and business are working together to build the South American Free Trade Agreement. Pressuring governments is complex; we can't appear to be interfering with their internal affairs. We have to show trust if we want an exchange of goods to occur."

While Steve evaded Joe's question, Theresa took pictures of Will out of her purse and laid them on the table. "This is Will Edwards," she said. She looked at each person at the table. They glanced at the pictures to avoid eye contact. "He's worth the world to me."

Steve slammed his hands down on the table and sat up in his chair. "I'm tired of being attacked and thought of as the bad guy. I've already made it clear to you, Mrs. Edwards, that we are doing what we can within the realm of the law. When you deal with governments and take the legal route, it takes time. Unfortunately, since the first hostage incident, laws have changed, and we prefer to leave the renegade tactics to the terrorists."

He stood up. "I believe we have reached an impasse," he said. "Further discussion would merely be repetitive." Rivers of rain raced down the length of the window. "Mrs. Edwards, gentlemen, I declare this meeting adjourned." The Blackburn executives and lawyers pushed their chairs away from the table and followed Steve out of the room.

Tears blurred Theresa's shaking hands as she gathered the pictures from the table. She wished she hadn't wasted Nick's money on the plane ticket. She hung onto her composure until the elevator doors closed and the video surveillance was off. Between sobs, she said to Joe, "I think they're just going to let him die."

Diamond Joe handed her a polka-dotted handkerchief. "You did just fine, Theresa. It was a good meeting. You showed them a face, and you reminded them that this man is a husband and a father, not just a case-in-file." He put a reassuring arm over her shoulders and pressed the GL button. Theresa was relieved to get back on ground level where people didn't need a lawyer's presence to tell the truth.

— — —

Theresa strapped herself into her airplane seat and watched the propellers turn. Rain rushed against her window. She wondered, *How could they possibly fly in this?*

Once they had reached cruising altitude, above the tumultuous clouds, Theresa relaxed the grip on her Styrofoam coffee cup and tried to roll the tension out of her shoulders. She needed to think about things.

She thought about Blackburn.

The company officials were able to divorce themselves from the humanity of the situation and absolve themselves from any responsibility. Sure, they cared enough to spend money on lawyers, but was that for Will's sake or theirs? In her opinion, Will didn't have as much time as the lawyers did. The world of Big Business made her feel as if her world was the abnormal one. Diamond Joe could navigate both worlds and interpret corporate doublespeak. He could hear what they *weren't* saying. He had said to her, "Blackburn Resources paid for a kidnapped man before; they never said they wouldn't pay again."

She thought about Foreign Affairs.

For three months, Theresa wondered why the department had seemed so ineffectual. Now she knew. Jim Itch's lectures were cribbed straight from Steve Steel's notes. Foreign Affairs didn't act in her best interests, but the company's. Theresa chided herself for not having seen the connection sooner. All along, she had fed information from Nick to Foreign Affairs, who then passed it on to Blackburn. Blackburn allowed Nick to do all the groundwork, while Foreign Affairs chastised him at the same time. Theresa now understood what Nick had known since day one. Neither Foreign Affairs nor Blackburn Resources International would get Will out of Colombia. Nick would.

Nick told her the government would never pay Will's ransom. He said our foreign policy was getting closer to the Americans' every day in that we agreed to make it illegal to talk to terrorists. Come to think of it, Jim Itch always called the guerrillas "terrorists" and always referred to the ransom as a "terrorist demand." With a free trade agreement pending, he didn't want her to make a fuss and turn a simple financial deal into something political. Theresa had accused Nick of exaggeration when he said governments like to create a state of fear so they could strip away democratic rights and control their citizens; she always thought *Nick* was the control freak. Theresa had always believed that people should be able to trust the integrity of their own government. But why was her phone bugged? And who was listening?

The airplane began its descent between the mountains.

She thought about Nick.

Something was going to happen. Soon. The last time she talked to Nick, he said that he thought the ARA was ready to make a deal. It upset Theresa that he had to liquidate his assets to raise ransom money. On the other hand, he hired Will, he told Will it was safe, and that's why Will was in Colombia. Her last conversation with Nick seemed odd because it had allowed her to glimpse a more personal side of him. Nick didn't usually bother much with small talk. What did Nick mean when he assured her that Will wouldn't be hurt? He told her that Ted would keep her posted. Did that mean *he* wouldn't? Why not? Where was he going? How dangerous were things in Colombia?

She thought about the media.

It was time to talk. What else could she do? She had to speak out against the injustice, damn it all, her husband was innocent. The *Ottawa Citizen* reporter would call her for details as soon as the *Monarch Valley Press* broke the story. She might even agree to interviews.

The landing gear dropped. Her jitters resurfaced and she held her breath until the airplane bumped onto the runway and came to a hurried stop in front of the terminal. She gave thanks a second time. The first was when she left the hectic Lower Mainland, destined for the interior of the province. By the time the seat belt sign stopped dinging, she had drawn her conclusion: she was on her own — she had to do whatever she could by herself. She had to be able to tell Kelly and Michael that she tried.

As she crossed the tarmac, Theresa saw Belinda waving exuberantly.

"Over here!" she called. "I borrowed Jan's Subaru. It's got four-wheel drive in case it snows. Don't worry about the van. Grease has it up on blocks again... not that it couldn't have made it."

Belinda opened the passenger door and Theresa fell in. The Subaru started on the third try. "How was your meeting?"

"Well, I don't think Will's going to call me from the phone booth in front of Dairy Queen tomorrow."

"Then you won't mind if some of us have been emailing Blackburn every day, asking about Will."

Theresa laughed. "Nope, don't mind at all."

"We're doing a few more things I should tell you about. Everyone wants to help, so we asked people to write to our MP. We gave out his address to the parents picking up their kids from Pat's day care. You know that day care bunch is a pretty subversive group." Belinda talked faster than the borrowed car could putter up the mountain road. "And people have been writing letters. We asked that all letters, faxes, and emails be copied to Foreign Affairs in Ottawa, attention: Jim Litchfield. Wherever they buried him."

Theresa smiled with her eyes closed.

"Frig!" Belinda exclaimed. "What is with these windshield wipers?" The rain beating against the windshield of the Subaru was turning into snow.

They came down from the mountain pass around a million curves until the car crossed Azure Creek leaving the rain and snow in the rear-view mirror. Theresa looked across the sleeping farmland to Monarch Valley with fondness, a feeling that lingered long after Belinda dropped her off at the house with the FOR SALE sign pounded into the front lawn.

TWENTY-SEVEN

THE LOUD BANGING against his door was not thunder. Instantly awake, Agustín heard the rain beating against his window and voices outside his door. Someone with the strength of a gorilla rattled his doorknob. Frozen in terror, he feared it was the DAS. Lightning flashed. He reached under his bed for his baseball bat and braced himself. Fortunately, Agustín checked his swing in time when the lock gave way and Nick and Alonso burst into his room at the same time as a booming clap of thunder. Muddy, bedraggled, and surprised by the bat, neither of them noticed the relief surge across Agustín's face as he set it down and flicked on the light.

Nick didn't wait for Agustín to put a shirt on before he blasted him for another "fuckin' failed mission." He and Alonso had just come down from the mountain where Agustín had directed them, but "one motherfuckin' mudslide" blocked the road, and it wouldn't be open until "bloody Mother-of-Mary Nature decided to fuckin' well reopen it," according to Nick. The rendezvous point was another five kilometres past the slide and Nick refused to hike the distance carrying a briefcase stuffed with bills. The slide looked fresh, Nick said, and as the weather worsened, he decided to leave before the next "son-of-a-bitchin'" storm moved in. Nick blamed Agustín for not checking the weather, and if he could have pinned the slide on him, he would have. Before they left, Nick threatened to "rattle more than just his fuckin' door if things didn't "fuckin'-well go right next fuckin' time."

Agustín was shaking. He wanted the hostage released and it hadn't happened. It was 2:45 AM and work started at 6:30. He fired up his computer to give Vanessa the details about the mudslide. She would already know the release had failed, but she wouldn't know why. If he could contact her, she could radio Constanza and tell him to stay put another day. Nick and Alonso could borrow his motorcycle to get around the slide. He stared at the blue screen. The power was on, but the Internet was not functioning. The telephone lines must be down. Agustín ran to the rain-spattered window and looked down at the wind shaking the trees in the park across the street. No telephone meant no communication with Vanessa, and that meant no communication with Constanza. He banged his head against the glass and closed his eyes. It just wasn't going to happen.

The following day, the telephone line hummed, but it was too late. Agustín read the email from Vanessa. The tone was vitriolic. Where had Nick been? Constanza waited all day and sent scouts down the mountain — no Nick. Vanessa reminded Agustín of the risk to the soldiers if the same release location was used too many times. Constanza would have to wait a week, maybe two, and then try again. The only good news in the message was that the severity of the storm prevented enemy surveillance, and the resistance cell left the camp undetected.

The payments Agustín received from the ARA allowed him to hire restaurant staff. His guerrilla-issue IBM computer gave him access to music, art, and newspapers from around the world. The computer had become an essential tool for sending and receiving communication beyond the walls of his country, and for emailing love notes to Mercedes.

Agustín apologized to Vanessa knowing that the explanation wouldn't change the outcome. He realized that one of the problems with Vanessa and the movement, was that communication only travelled one way.

— — —

It was 9:35 PM on October 5. Nick inhaled the smoke from his cigarette as he tilted back in his T-Rex office chair. He liked his chair despite its farting noises and rude squawks. Solidly built from a species of tropical hardwood that probably didn't exist anymore, the chair's arms were moulded to his arms, and the seat cushion had just the right amount of plump to it. Moths circled the lamp that shed light on a desk cluttered with a torn map, a calculator, three full ashtrays, a rotary telephone with a curly cord, stacks of hundred dollar US bills, and loose papers covered with columns of figures. Despite Hector's promissory note, Nick's numbers wouldn't match the ransom. He refused to take the money Theresa offered.

In two months, Nick had sold five years' worth of company assets. The trucks went easily; he got an okay price for his camp equipment and mobile wash house. It really jarred him that Blackburn got a hell of a deal on his D-8 caterpillar. Nick spooked Alonso when he told him that bodyguards were fetching a good price on the Internet. Alonso laughed uneasily.

Nick snapped elastic bands around the bills and piled them into his briefcase branded with the "T-Rex of Timmins — Colombia

Division" logo. Nick did not intend to give up Alonso. When the law of the jungle rules, and a man is about to enter said space with a bulging briefcase cuffed to his wrist, Alonso was hardly a frivolous accessory.

— — —

At 10 PM on the same day, three taxi drivers conversed quietly as they leaned against their cars at the entrance of the *Parque Central* in the *ciudad vieja* district. Across the street, a blue light shone from a second-floor room of the Hotel California.

Vanessa's curt email did not surprise Agustín. In fact, it sounded friendly compared to the one she sent him ten days ago. Relations had been less than ideal since then. Tonight's message from Vanessa confirmed his suspicions. The exchange would occur tomorrow, October 6. Agustín noted the change in location. He powered down the computer, pulled the cord from the modem, and plugged into the telephone. He called Nick at his office on Calle San Miguel and forwarded Vanessa's message verbally: Meet the captive at the mudslide.

Agustín stared at the telephone after he hung up. He admired Nick for his staunch loyalty to his worker. A long time ago, it was the ARA's concern for the worker that impressed him. Now the ARA was punishing Nick for the same virtue it claimed to uphold. Agustín wanted to be free of this mission and looked forward to dissolving his association with the movement. His future commitments depended upon a clean background, or at least, keeping his past connections hidden.

Following the national election this past June, the People's Democratic Party of Colombia had approached Mercedes. She decided to throw her bulletproof bonnet into the electoral ring. She had the money, intelligence, good looks, and confidence needed to win. What she lacked were connections, something Agustín viewed as an advantage over the present representative. In his opinion, the country needed a governing body where people with integrity, not connections, ran for office. Agustín had always assumed that if you gave the people someone decent to vote for, they would respond. The political route would be a long-term project, but Agustín shared his girlfriend's dream of a better Colombia. He agreed to help with her campaign because she was what his country needed. He suggested that her clothing factory supply her wardrobe.

— — —

At 10:15 PM, Nick set the receiver down and dribbled cigarette ashes across the floor to a saucer that sat on the counter. He hadn't slept much lately, and he was too tired to drive to Rose's. Besides, Alonso was probably asleep in the truck and he didn't want to wake him. They needed to get an early start tomorrow.

He decided to sack out on the wooden floor of his tiny office and use his chair cushion for a pillow. He handcuffed his briefcase to his arm before he pulled the chain on his lamp. The security guard that used to patrol the premises was long gone, and the broken locks hadn't been repaired. Since the auction, there was nothing left to guard in the warehouse, and without the photocopier and the fax machine, little remained in the office. Except this chair, with its patterned cushion. And Nick was right on top of that.

TWENTY-EIGHT

"YOU'VE GOT TO JUMP HIGHER!"

"You've got to be quicker!"

"You've got to run faster!" The soldiers playing cards at Camp Coffee urged Will on as he crashed through the coffee bushes in pursuit of the blue butterfly, swinging his ballcap in every direction.

Since his vision a week ago, Will's need to catch the butterfly surpassed his need to eat, to drink, to sleep, and even his need to escape. When he returned to the card game empty-hatted, Francisco warned Will that the insect had cast a spell over him. Will agreed. "If I'd have found my own horseshoe, I'd be gone by now," he said. "But since Luis and José left, I've had lots of time to think. The butterfly is the luck I need to get back home."

"Why don't you use your coveralls to catch the butterfly instead of your little hat?" suggested Juan looking up from his cards.

"That's a good idea." He crawled into his tent to retrieve them. The next time he'd be ready.

— — —

On the 102nd day of his confinement, Will captured the butterfly. He had swiped at the creature with his coveralls and then couldn't find it. But when he shook them out, the insect wafted down like a feather and landed on the toe of his yellow boot. He bent down and cradled it in his rough hands, closing his eyes in thanks. Will looked at its still body and thought it was the most magical thing he had ever held. He brought his hands to his lips and breathed warm, moist air into them until he felt a slight flutter. As the movement got stronger, Will considered the creature in his hands. It was a wild thing, made from the blue of the sky. Will walked toward the coffee bushes and opened his hands. In return for its freedom, the butterfly gave him a promise. Will reached into his breast pocket and brought out his photos. He dusted his hands so that the blue powder fell over the faces of Kelly, Michael, and Theresa. He then returned his pictures to the pocket over his heart. As his ancestors had worn the claws, the feathers, and the pelts of animals respected and learned from, he would carry the promise of freedom given to him by the butterfly.

— — —

El Capitán's sciatica limited the length of his stride and caused him to drag one leg. "No more fucking around," he told Simón Bolívar Juárez as he rolled up the antenna wire. "Tell the soldiers we leave for the bamboo forest at dawn."

— — —

In early October, McIntosh apples fetched a good price. The larch trees on the mountain had turned from green to gold. The house on Copper Crescent with the FOR SALE sign sat behind a confusion of household items. Theresa hauled stuff out of the house while Kelly sat at a card table taking money and Michael hauled other stuff back in. Theresa thought a garage sale might divert her attention away from the hundred-and-second X on her kitchen calendar. That, combined with full-time work, Michael's hockey practices, arguing with Kelly over her high school's dress code, making salsa, picking plums, raking leaves, winterizing the house and garden, and accepting invitations to attend Thanksgiving dinner. All of these diversions helped.

— — —

Agustín transferred the glowing charcoal from the wood-burning oven to the grill with a long-handled paddle and laid the meat flat on the grill. He cooked the Argentine beef, Ted's favourite, while Ted and Uncle Oscar watched *fútbol* on TV. Uncle Oscar seemed satisfied when Agustín explained that the men in suits with an unhealthy curiosity were auditors. Fortunately, he had deleted several files, documents, and messages prior to their arrival. He was also thankful that Sebastian's had survived its first six months and now claimed a business-class following. Its success fuelled Agustín's dream of an eco-tourist lodge on the coast. One day.

— — —

Alonso drove the pick-up too fast up the mountain road while Nick smoked. Trees blocked the view of the precipice below. The briefcase, a map, a rifle, a box of cartridges, cigarettes, a backpack full of provisions, binoculars, and a camera bounced around inside the cab like Mexican jumping beans. Agustín's motorcycle was strapped in the truck box. When the road started disintegrating beneath their wheels, they stopped. Nick cut some branches to conceal the truck while Alonso backed the bike down the single-plank ramp. Nick climbed aboard and they travelled the remaining distance by motorcycle. When they reached the mudslide, they waited, watched, smoked, and listened.

A pack and a half later, Alonso heard a whine slightly louder than the ubiquitous mosquitoes. They ducked into the shrubbery. Alonso adjusted the rifle on his shoulder and spied the approaching motorcycle through the scope. Nick watched through the binoculars. Once he got a clear view of the riders dressed in camouflage, a rifle slung over the passenger's back, and a headscarf on the driver, he made himself visible. The riders puttered up to the slide about a hundred metres away, and turned off the engine.

Nick shouted across the mudslide, "*Donde esta el cautivo?*"

The one with the rifle replied, "*Donde esta el dinero?*"

Nick held up his arm and the attached briefcase. No one moved. "*No hombre, no dinero!*" he shouted. He turned toward his motorcycle. Alonso stepped out of the green with the rifle still on his shoulder, ready to fire. The guerrillas turned their bike around and talked into a radio.

Minutes passed. Alonso eyed the Che Guevara bandana through the scope of his rifle. He could hold this position for days if he had to. Nick leaned against the bike.

The guerrilla without the headscarf held up a hand and said in a boy's voice, "*Espérenme aquí!*" *Wait here.* Then the small bike whined back up the mountain.

Nick and Alonso smoked the rest of their pack as morning turned into afternoon.

— — —

Francisco and Juan returned to Mosquito Camp and reported to El Capitán. Will sat in front of his tent without his socks or yellow boots on. He played with a mass of something squishy that gurgled under the skin of his foot. It moved around when he pushed it. The size of the mass had increased tenfold since walking up the mountain, and the colour had changed. Will tried to move the thing to a place on his foot where it wouldn't rub on his boot, so he was unresponsive when El Capitán blocked his light.

"Get your things together. Leave the army gear here. Your friend is waiting."

This was the moment he had waited one hundred and five days for. He sat in disbelief, holding his foot.

El Capitán jabbed his finger toward the ground, "*Ahora!*"

Will jumped into his crusty socks and pulled on his boots. They weren't as bright as they used to be, and the bottoms were as smooth as ripe mangoes. He left the army gear, the groundsheet, and his coveralls in a heap by the tent. With staff in hand, he stood where Luis and José had stood sixty-five days ago. Francisco approached him to say farewell. Will grinned through a black beard, his eyes bright and alive.

"*Adios, y buena suerte, Señor Eduardo — hombre viejo.*"

Will shook Francisco's hand. "Call me when you get to Canada, Frank. I don't think my wife will let me come back here."

El Capitán barked and Will obeyed for the last time. He looked back at the other soldiers watching him and touched his hat in an off-kilter salute. Zhuri waved. The watch on her wrist fell nearly to her elbow. The second-in-command started walking down the mountain. Will hustled after him.

Fifteen minutes down the trail they uncovered a yellow Kawasaki motorcycle. The second-in-command hauled the bike into an upright position, got on, and kicked it into action. Will climbed on behind, and stuffed his snake-killing staff in his boot. With all nine and a half fingers gripping the controls, the second-in-command chauffeured a grinning Will down the bumpy trail.

When the Kawasaki stopped at the mudslide, Will saw two men on the other side. He rolled off the bike while the second-in-command held on, and clambered over the conglomerate of boulders, stumps, and tree trunks to the other side. He barely needed his staff.

A small, wiry man with bushy eyebrows and a briefcase walked toward Will. He extended his free hand. "I'm Nick Nordstrom. Let's just call this a shift change. You've got a family that wants you home." Despite his weariness, Will's eyes sparkled as he wrung the man's hand.

Alonso snapped their picture. The two men embraced. Will knew the voice, but he had never seen Nick in person before. He held the much smaller man at arm's length to get a good look at him.

"So you're Nick," he said. "I've been waiting to meet you for a long time. A very long time."

Nick introduced Alonso. Will, still grinning, pumped Alonso's hand up and down. Will asked about his brother and if anyone had spoken to Theresa lately. Both men nodded, and then Nick asked Will some questions about the guerrilla camp. After a few short and precious minutes, the second-in-command waved his pistol, reminding everyone why the party had been called.

Nick slid his pack over the shoulder. Will and Alonso watched Nick, with the briefcase locked to his wrist, walk across the mudslide towards the guerrilla soldier. Once across, the second-in-command gestured to him to open the case. Nick reached into his pocket for the key, unlocked his wrist, and opened the briefcase. The second-in-command thumbed through the bills, often casting a watchful eye in Alonso's direction. Will didn't think he looked pleased. He couldn't hear the second-in-command's questions or Nick's answers.

Will could sense how uneasy Alonso felt without his rifle in his hand. He watched as he laid the camera on the ground and reached for the weapon lying nearby. The second-in-command saw him as well. A pistol flashed, and a bullet zinged past Alonso. The sound carried a long way through the mountain valley. Will's ears rang. It was the loudest sound he'd heard in three months. Alonso froze. He and Will watched the second-in-command point his pistol at Nick and move toward the Kawasaki. The second-in-command motioned for Alonso and Will to leave. If Alonso were to try anything with the rifle, Nick would surely die. Alonso cared too much for Nick to take that chance, so he and Will climbed aboard their motorcycle. Will looked back at Nick, who was now astride the Kawasaki holding onto his briefcase.

The pair rode down the mountain. Will shed tears of happiness but couldn't see the tears of sadness in Alonso's eyes. In the distance, across the mudslide, they could hear the Kawasaki whine back up the mountain trail.

TWENTY-NINE

"I DIDN'T SEE IT COMING," Alonso told Will as they cleared the brush away from the truck. "Nick said the money was a little short, but he told me he figured the guerrillas would agree to the deal." Will could see the big man was engulfed in grief and disbelief.

As Alonso rode the motorcycle up the plank into the truck box, Will opened the passenger door and climbed in, as if climbing back onboard the spinning planet. Nick's exchange had turned the flavour of his freedom bittersweet — the burden of a man's confinement was now his to bear.

"Nick always looks out for his friends," Alonso said.

Will sat, proof of Alonso's statement. His freedom didn't make up for the loss of Alonso's boss and friend. "He's a brave man," he said. "I don't know if I would willingly walk into a guerrilla camp."

As the truck rumbled down the mountain, Will's anxiety increased. He had no papers. "You're sure there aren't any roadblocks?"

"Not unless they've stuck something up on Highway 22 since this morning." Alonso was more surprised than Will when they hit the military checkpoint. They were still about two hours away from Bucaramanga. Two armed guards in military uniform stood in front of a wooden barricade across the road.

Will was aware how scruffy he looked. He hadn't shaved for more than a hundred days, and his clothes were dirty. He began to shake; sweat soaked his collar. The military would demand proof of his identity — which of course he didn't have. If he were to tell the truth, they would escort him into the city for questioning. That would take time that Will, now a free man, did not have. It was the greatest fear he'd experienced in all of his days in Colombia.

"Don't say a word," Alonso whispered as he pulled the truck up to the barricade. The military men motioned them to get out. Will obeyed, turned around, and placed his hands on the truck. He stared at his fingers, caked in dirt. While Will's guard searched him and rifled through the truck, Alonso and his guard talked motorcycles. How many ccs. How fast. Chrome. Tires. The uniformed man held up his arms "chopper style" and pretended to rev the engine. Alonso's head nodded, appearing to share his enthusiasm.

Alonso took the guard around to the back of the truck and set up the ramp. He climbed up into the box and eased the bike down the narrow plank. When it roared to life, the guard looked at the other guard and smiled broadly. Alonso turned the ignition off and parked the bike next to the barricade. He turned his back on the military men and climbed into the truck. Will did the same. No more questions.

Alonso fumed and expressed his disgust with the military, while Will gripped the handle above the door. He could not relax. He'd spent one hundred and five days with the guerrillas. The last thing he wanted was to spend another hundred and five with the military.

The reckless driving, the speed, the noise and commotion, the traffic, the garbage, the shops, the crowds of people, all gave Will a sensory overload once they crossed the city limits. He wanted to clap his hands over his ears and squeeze his eyes shut. Bucaramanga seemed a faster and noisier city than the one he departed from last June.

A red sun shone at a low angle through the city's dust and diesel fumes as Alonso parked in front of the Hotel California. Will gradually released the handle above the truck door. In four hours he had travelled from the Stone Age to *Star Wars*. He looked at the coral-coloured stucco of the two-storey hotel and the neon sign that spelled Sebastian's. A phone call home, a shower, a shave, and maybe a cold beer or two with Ted were among the luxuries he wouldn't have allowed himself to consider as recently as twenty-four hours ago. Now he could do it whenever he wanted, and in any order. It was his call.

As he climbed stiffly out of the truck, his brother charged toward him. They embraced in a giant whooping bear hug. The browner, thinner, dirtier, smellier, and hairier Will spoke first. "You look like you've been well taken care of."

Ted laughed. "And you look thin — I bet you could use a good meal!"

"Yeah, my belt doesn't fit me anymore, but I wouldn't recommend the diet."

With arms over each other's shoulders, they walked into Sebastian's to meet an ebullient Oscar and a politely smiling Agustín. They all shook hands, laughed, and cried in disbelief when Alonso described the exchange. No one could have known. In a country where survival depends upon one's ability to keep a secret, Nick's bold action commanded respect. The first glass was raised in his honour.

Before a second glass could be downed, Ted offered Will his room upstairs. "It has a shower with water that runs out of a tap and a toilet that flushes. Most of the time."

"What about a phone?"

"Yes, that too. It knows your number, in case you've forgotten."

Out of the brightness of the restaurant, Ted led his big brother up the hotel's back stairway, which was still short on light and in need of fumigation. To Will, it was the Hollywood Hilton.

Will found the telephone under a crumple of newspapers in Ted's room. He picked up the receiver and listened to the monotonous hum — what an incredible invention! He did remember the number. One ring... a moth singed its wings on the bare lightbulb. Two rings... he looked where his watch used to be to determine the time in Monarch Valley.

"Hello?"

"Hi, Cookie."

"Will, is that really you?"

"Yeah. It is. I'm sorry, Theresa."

Even after months of longing and visualizing the woman he dreamed about a million miles away, he didn't have much to say. He had caused her so much pain. Tears robbed him of words. He just wanted her to talk to him. So she did.

— — —

Agustín cooked chicken and fried potato chips for the celebration that included Oscar, Alonso, the reunited brothers, several hotel patrons, and whoever else from the general public showed up. Mercedes tended the nonstop bar. Spanish champagne tangoed with Caribbean rum as it spilled across the tiled floor. The celebration resembled a wake and a wedding all at once. Beverages were consumed in the traditional South American manner: All night long. For the first time in many months, Will slept in a bed with a roof over his head. He fell asleep so quickly that he failed to notice the comfort of a stained and sagging mattress.

— — —

Yellow, brown, and red leaves swirled in the streets of Monarch Valley. The biggest change, Will noted, was that the road to Copper Crescent had been paved. Some work needed to be done around the house and garden, but with so many people coming to visit, he didn't know if that would happen anytime soon. He would have to call Jerry to come and pick up his FOR SALE sign. He planned to replace it with a tall pole and a Canadian flag.

He called Nick's family and associates in Timmins and talked about what Nick might be experiencing. Ted remained in Colombia, where he enjoyed more friends and less rain than at home in Vancouver. He, Alonso, and Agustín were working out a plan between the ARA, a Catholic priest, and Blackburn on behalf of Nick. Their work was just beginning.

— — —

"There's a new *Star Wars* movie and I have to show you my hockey cards. I'm only missing the Canucks goalie, but Peter has two, and he'll trade me for my Trevor Linden. I can always get another Trevor Linden. It would be so cool to have the whole team." Unlike the other Edwards men, Michael had no shortage of words. "And Dad, don't call me Michael anymore. I'm Mike."

The changes in Kelly were more dramatic. Will realized that she was still a young girl on the inside, but on the outside ... was she wearing makeup? She certainly liked the emerald earrings he bought her.

As for Theresa, her smile was much brighter, her eyes much bigger, and her legs much longer than he remembered. Much softer and smoother too. One long-stemmed Colombian rose would arrive every day for the next one hundred and five days. Until then, they had a bit of catching up to do before the next Thanksgiving invitation — for four — appeared.

THIRTY

NICK SIPPED HIS COLOMBIAN COFFEE from Will's mug as he sat in front of Will's tent, wishing like hell he had a cigarette. He watched the soldiers, counted rifles, and contemplated escape. According to his Spanish, he had overheard one soldier tell another that a whole new battalion of young revolutionaries would soon replace the present group. So, he thought, if he were going to spring himself, sooner would be better than later. He'd skirt around this ragged coffee plantation and follow the creek to the river.

His guard and three more soldier boys played cards. Funny, Nick thought to himself, they're playing gin rummy. Nick eyed the rifles stacked like a tripod an arm's length away from the cardplayers. His gaze moved to the two soldier girls washing clothes at the stream. They paid him no mind as they stretched the garments out flat on the sunny rocks. Where were their rifles? Farther down-stream, Nick liked the looks of the other two soldier girls cleaning the lunch dishes, even though one was a little too butch for his taste. Their rifles were also too far away. The miserable bastard who had led him back to camp disappeared somewhere with the supply mule in tow. Hell, Nick figured, these guys gotta get their jollies one way or another. From his vantage point, Nick could see the commander through a screen of greenery, enjoying an afternoon siesta in his hammock, seemingly at peace with the world. What a relief, thought Nick. That head honcho was one tense bastard.

It had been three days since the exchange, and Christ, was he sore. The morning after he "volunteered" for this job, they made him hike for an entire day and half the night. How in hell had Will done this? The guy was no spring chicken. Temporarily distracted by two blue butterflies fluttering across the camp clearing, Nick wondered how much of a lead he could get if he made a run for it now, and whether there were any crocs in the river.

— — —

Zhuri and Jenny scrubbed the rice pots with sedge grass that grew next to the stream. In a few days, their tour of duty would be over.

"I can't go back to the farm," Jenny said. "I need to get away and live my own life."

"I'm going back to Pamplona. I miss my mother. As for my fa-ther... well, I think I can work things out with him. Vicente won't be around and I've been giving a lot of thought to our relationship. When he gets out, we'll see what happens. Where will you go?"

"The capital. My brother and his family live there. Isobel should have had her baby by now. They're really hoping for a boy this time — me too. I have three nieces already. I can help with the kids or work Isobel's shift until she goes back to the factory." Jenny glanced at her reflection in the cooking pot. "I'm sure glad you helped me learn to read."

"There are libraries in the city you can go to," Zhuri said. "You have to read *One Hundred Years of Solitude*. Believe me, it's a better story than *Das Kapital*."

"You should be a teacher, Zhuri. If I'd had someone like you, I probably would have stayed in school."

"I can't believe they call the propaganda here a 'classroom.' There's a difference between education and indoctrination. Anyway, I'd like to finish school at home and then go to university in Bucaramanga. I can stay with my brother and help him with his restaurant."

"Good luck. I know you will do good — I mean, do well."

"Thanks, Jenny. Here." Zhuri removed Will's watch and gave it to Jenny. "This is for helping me be a better soldier. If you didn't carry half my load, I'd have fallen over backward. Besides, it's a little big on me." She showed Jenny how to work all of its functions. Jenny liked the button on the side that gave the face an aqua glow. She slipped the watch on and both girls admired the fit. Jenny blushed. She had little practice in saying thank you.

— — —

The sound of the stream and the intensity of the card game may have prevented the guerrillas from hearing the helicopters. By the time they did, it was too late for anything but a desperate scattering. Angela and Maria grabbed the clothes from the rocks. Zhuri and Jenny threw tarps over the food, dishes, and the shiny cooking pot. Francisco manhandled Nick into the coffee bushes and pushed him down. No time for blankets. The commander mouthed orders that went unheard over the sound of the helicopters.

From his position in the bushes, Nick felt the group's panic. Orders directed at him were unintelligible. Just confused noise. Nick's heart raced. He'd make a run for it amid the disarray. He looked toward the creek to see which way if flowed. Jesus Christ, was that rapid fire? Francisco fell backward into the coffee bushes bloodied by the blast of machine-gun fire from above. Nick's adrenaline kicked in as he ran away on spring-loaded legs. Bullets like miniature dust devils skipped across the clearing. The helicopter reeled above them, hovering, turning, firing round after round. Two more of the guerrillas — Nick never learned their names — lay dead in the clearing. The grey belly of a second helicopter loomed overhead, whipping and tearing tree branches. The guerrillas' bullets pinged off their giant steel bodies. Nick could taste the metallic throb of the helicopter. His jawbone rattled with it, and his heart beat to it. As he charged through the coffee plants, he felt invisible — his captors couldn't see him, lost in their own frantic firing and loading and firing and running.

The confusion of stampeding soldiers, whirling helicopter blades, and machine-gun fire ravaged the coffee bushes, the corn plants, the nut trees, and the shade trees, as if everything had been caught in a cyclone. When Nick burst through the bushes onto the flat rocks where the girls had washed the clothes, he met a hovering Black Hawk, puking out its squadron of army men, guns raised and ready to fire. He stopped dead, then ran back the way he had come. He hunched down and darted across the clearing. Playing cards fluttered randomly, as confused as the dust that swirled and churned in front of him. The queen of spades lifted up and then drifted down. It landed on the unseeing eye of the girl with the long black braid. Nick was caught in the middle. Was it a guerrilla bullet, or an army bullet? It stung like a hornet, but he limped away from the pain until a shot to his head exploded in his brain and brought him down.

The fire continued from the helicopter in the sky and from the militia on the ground. Bullet spray shredded the tents and blasted the tarps to tatters. The camp kitchen disintegrated. Camouflaged guerrilla bodies became part of the lifeless wreckage.

The army soldiers mustered in the centre of the clearing that was once Camp Coffee.

A peculiar rain began to fall — peculiar because there were no clouds, and the sky was blue. There was no thunder, no lightning. The drops that fell were not wet, but dry and powdery. And blue. Pieces of blue butterfly drifted down from the tattered trees and the silent sky. The pieces covered the torn ground, blanketed the spoiled coffee bushes, and shrouded the young bodies. Factory-made bullets from America, from Venezuela, from Russia, perfectly designed to kill, lay buried by blue scales from the most beautiful of the world's butterflies.

— — —

AUTHOR'S AFTERWORD

Butterflies in Bucaramanga is a fictional story based on real people and true events.

On June 24, 1998, Ed Leonard of Creston, B.C. was kidnapped from his work camp in northeast Colombia and held captive for 105 days by leftist guerrillas.

Trollee Leonard works at the Creston Optometric Eye Centre and is a good friend. While Ed was held hostage, she was frustrated by the lack of information and hurt by the apparent lack of compassion from Canadian Foreign Affairs and the Canadian mining company responsible for worker protection. Trollee did not receive any news about her husband until August, when a fax providing proof of life was sent by his drill boss in Colombia.

Norbert Reinhart, owner of an Ontario-based drilling company, was Ed's drill boss. Norbert and Ed's brother Joe maintained contact with Trollee from Bucaramanga. Fuelled by a sense of social justice and stonewalled by the diplomatic process, Norbert contacted the guerrillas himself in order to negotiate a ransom. Reinhart's actions overstepped international protocol and remain controversial. While the character of Nick Nordstrom was inspired by Reinhart, he is my own fictional creation.

Any resemblance to other real-life individuals in this book is coincidental. The guerrillas in the story are fictional characters derived from research. Colombia's real-life guerrillas, however, are a part of history, with a voice that deserves to be heard.

Colombia is a country with a rich culture, a diverse ecology, and a complex history, and filled with friendly people. Hopefully, more peaceful times await them in the future. My descriptions of Colombia are based on places I visited and butterflies I saw in neighbouring countries.

It was a privilege to work with Ed and Trollee Leonard. I felt that they had given me a precious story that needed to be written down. Ed was a natural storyteller and often told friends his stories over a glass of dark rum. Fortunately, thanks to the Creston Library, he recorded his true experiences on compact disc prior to his passing in August of 2009. The memory of a gentle, soft-spoken man and his story lives on.

ACKNOWLEDGMENTS

Michael Hingston — NeWest Press editor, a man as sharp a his pencil.

Luanne Armstrong — structural and line editor, supporter of all Kootenay writers

Writers' Group — Deryn Collier, Kuya Minogue, Kelly Ryckman, Ilana Cameron

Betsy Brierley — substantive editor and fan of Eats, Shoots & Leaves

Gene Zackowski — unwavering support

Sebastian Zackowski — listener and reader

Connie MacDonald, Genevieve Patterson, Jan Zackowski — readers

Holly Pender-Love — the catalyst

Brenda Loftus and Chief Chris Luke Sr. — advisors on native issues

Kim Asquith — Girl Guide leader

Fernando and staff at Cabinas Colibri, Playa Carrillo, Costa Rica — restaurant setting

Sandra Rubio — my Colombian connection

Byron Wilson — motorcycle guy

Frank Wishlow — computer guy

Joe and Katherine at Kingfisher Books — books, reading venue, and chai tea providers

Robert Michael Pyle and Ed McMackin — lepidopterists (everyone should know one)

Gilbert Across-the-Mountain — who lent me his name

Ann Day, Pat Tomasik, Darla Grewal — Creston librarians

Jon Krakauer — for the initial telephone call

Jesús Abad Colorado — exiled Colombian photojournalist who provided inspiration

María Hortencia Bussiere and Victor Guardado — Spanish language guides

Exchange students — Agustín (Argentina), Zhuri (Peru), Uli (Germany), Damien (France)

People of Creston, B.C., our office staff, and Leonard family, friends, and relations.

TANNA PATTERSON-Z has a B.A. in Environmental

Studies from the University of Waterloo and a Renewable Resources Diploma from Lakeland College in Vermilion, Alberta. Her first book, *Exploring the Creston Valley*, published in 1989 by Waterwheel Press, is a guide to hiking, bicycling, and canoeing in the Creston Valley. She has also dabbled in children's stories and contributed articles to the *Creston Valley Advance* and the newsletter of the conservation group, Wildsight. Her father Claude, and her teacher-librarian mom, Genevieve, gave her a life-long love for books. She shares the Kootenay lifestyle with her husband Gene, two grown sons Jan and Sebastian.

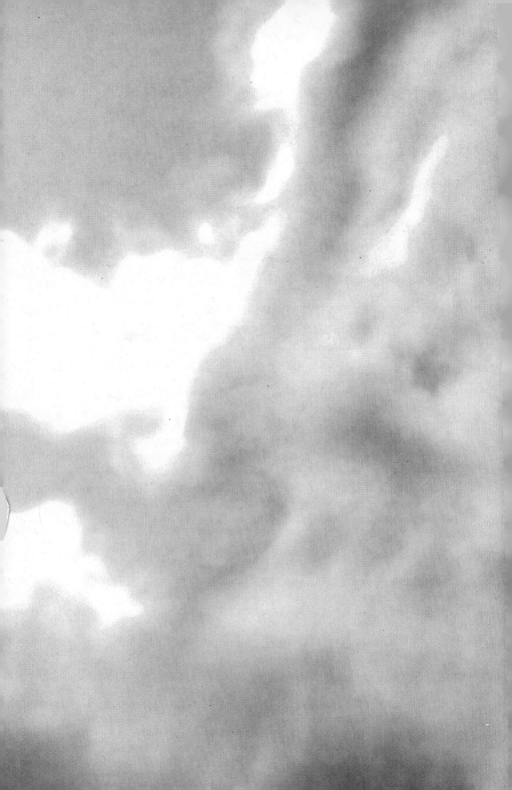